Tales of Dusty Death

Tales of Dusty Death

Jane Hayward

Matador
9 Priory Business Park,
Wistow Road, Kibworth Beauchamp,
Leicestershire., LE8 0RX
Tel: 0116 279 2299
Email: books@troubador.co.uk
Web: www.troubador.co.uk/matador
Twitter: @matadorbooks

ISBN 978 1800460 522

British Library Cataloguing in Publication Data.
A catalogue record for this book is available from the British Library.

Printed and bound in Great Britain by 4edge Limited
Typeset in 11pt Adobe Garamond Pro by Troubador Publishing Ltd, Leicester, UK

Matador is an imprint of Troubador Publishing Ltd

I should like to thank Dave Swann, my tutor during the short story module at Chichester University; three writing colleagues from those days, Clare Brown, Annie Thomson and Melanie Walker, who still support me by reading my drafts, editing and commenting on them and, finally, my husband Peter, who, with great patience always reads, comments, advises on and edits my work.

Tomorrow, and tomorrow, and tomorrow,
Creeps in this petty pace from day to day,
To the last syllable of recorded time;
And all our yesterdays have lighted fools
The way to dusty death.

Macbeth act 5 scene 5

Contents

Foreword

I began by writing short stories aimed at the women's magazine market. Nil success.

Then I read in a book that writing novels was easier than writing short stories. At least it seemed easier. I achieved a modest success.

During my MA in Creative Writing at Chichester University we followed a module on the short story. I wrote a story which was published in the Lightship Anthology 1 by Alma Press. The story is included in this collection under the title *A Fish out of Water*.

When I wrote the Fish story, I hadn't intended it to be in the magic realism genre nor to end in death. Based on holiday memories of a Tuscan villa, the landscape and the local hill-top village, Monte San Savino, I wrote. The story grew and developed.

Short stories take years to write. Not days, or weeks or months. Years.

JH 2020

Dressed for a Party

I didn't want Mother in church wearing her old cotton nightie. She'd be out of that box like a banshee. I wanted her body looking its old self. Clutching my carrier bag, I pushed open the door of Winston & Winston – Funerals and Cremations.

I promised myself, whatever I was asked, I would not shed a tear.

He was dressed in a navy suit and red tie. My grey mac felt shabby, not good enough. Mother would have said, 'You do wear some odd clothes sometimes.' I hadn't got round to buying a new coat. There's a great deal to do when someone dies. Shopping is hardly at the top of the list.

He took the bag, looked inside and nodded at me. 'Often the bereaved forget the underclothes.'

I was pleased. Mother would be proud of me.

Stylish, Mother was. Good bones, deep-set eyes, fully curved lips. She only went two days ago. I sat with her as the colour drained from her face; watched her body chill out of being my mum and stiffen into a corpse. I was shocked by how quickly she was gone for ever. There was no doubt about it. Death is the end.

Still, both of us had to attend the final reception and, determined Mother would be smartly dressed, I had chosen her wool crepe dress and jacket. She often wore black for formal occasions, even though the colour didn't flatter her. That was where the red shoes came in. I stared at them in my hand, fixed on them as if I had only just discovered them, as if I had never watched them taking Mother to social occasions.

'These are her shoes. Red court. Mother wore them to parties.'

Remembering Mother wearing them, I almost smiled. How she loved her get-togethers, giving them or going to them. Death was too still for both of us.

As he took the shoes, the undertaker's face told me nothing, his eyes didn't widen in amazement nor his lips in amusement. He said, 'These shoes don't match her suit.'

Which made me cross. What did he know about Mother? I snapped at him which I didn't mean to. 'Matching never bothered her. It won't now.' I thrust my hand into my pocket and pulled out a string of beads. 'And she's to wear these.' A jet and marcasite necklace: long, 1920s style. Some would say it was a waste to bury it, but not me. It was the last rites after all and I reckoned after living this hard life, a person deserved the best. I gave him the beads, slipping them from my fingers onto his palm. No touching.

He raised his eyebrows and, just at that minute, I didn't trust him. The necklace couldn't have been valuable. Mother didn't have much money. 'I'd like her to look…'

'Finished?' he suggested.

I nodded. Finishing was what I had in mind.

'Will you…?' I felt stupid and hesitated. Why was it so difficult to talk about the end? I concentrated on the surface of his desk, green leather with a gold trim. Who'd want to imagine her own mother being seen naked by a strange man? Especially once she's dead. 'Will you be looking after her?'

'My wife takes care of that side of things. For the ladies, naturally.'

I looked at him then. 'Naturally.'

He wanted to know if I'd be back to see Mother. When she was ready.

I couldn't hide the tremor in my voice. 'I'll ring, shall I and see if you... if your wife has...?'

'Finished.'

I was back the next day with a pair of black boots. The soles were peeling at the toes although the heels were freshly shod. The leather of the uppers was split in a couple of places but not enough to let water in and the laces were broken and knotted together. The boots had metal hooks to wind the laces round. Depending upon the age of the person wearing them, they were either old-fashioned or bang up-to-date. That morning, I'd thrown them in the wheelie bin and slammed the lid shut. Two minutes later and I was fishing them out.

The previous winter, I'd taken Mother to buy new boots. Even I found the experience confusing. We stared into the shop window at bright blue shoes with thick clumpy heels and sandals with straps so thin you could bite through them. We saw white, shiny boots not strong enough to weather a shower let alone snow. We gazed at evening shoes with sparkles on, beach shoes with flowers on and tennis shoes with gold stripes on.

Mother said, 'I thought we came for boots.'

Then we saw some. Right back in the far corner of the window, as though someone had added them as an afterthought, were a pair of brown, lace-up boots. Mother commented she always wore black. I suggested a different colour would make a change. Brown would match your beige coat, I told her. We both became obstinate. Mother said her handbag was black; I suggested we buy a new one. A brown one.

'I like the boots I'm wearing', said Mother, rolling her lips tightly, pressing them together until they looked hard.

In the shop, she squatted on a low chair as a young person wearing gardeners' overalls helped her untie the old fastenings on her boots and then took the new boots from the window. 'Would Madam like to try them on?'

Mother said, 'It's my daughter who thinks I need new boots, but it's not my daughter paying, is it? Do you force your mother to buy things she doesn't want?' She turned to me, her face puce with anger. 'There's nothing wrong with these boots.'

Then she pulled on her tatty black boots, stood up and, leaving the laces dangling, marched out of the shop to jump on the next bus home.

⫷⫸

Now, here I was, standing in the street, summoning up the courage to enter the funeral parlour. I pushed the door open. He was there, waiting for me. I spoke in a rush of words. My mouth trembled while my eyelids blinked. 'I can't throw these in the bin.'

'You gave me the courts. Do you want her to wear these instead?'

I shook my head. 'She'll be dressed for an occasion. She wore these every day. I tried to get her to buy a new pair once but she wouldn't. She could be quite difficult, my mother.' A choke in my throat interrupted my words and I had to blink my lashes very quickly. I felt a cup of tea was in order.

He understood and took me into a back room, away from the window onto the street. He brought a tray, the full works: tea-pot, two cups and saucers, milk in a little jug and sugar in a bowl. I'm not the mug and tea-bag type.

'It's not uncommon to have the odd difference with a parent,' he said. 'Especially as the years get on.'

I nodded. I couldn't stop myself talking. 'Mother should have let me buy her a new pair of boots. These are a disgrace. I suggested it but Mother rolled her lips together. I knew what she was going to say.'

'What was that?'

'That it was a ridiculous suggestion and she was having none of it. There's nothing wrong with these, that's what Mother said. Nothing wrong with them? They're falling to bits.' I tried laughing but it was a thin, high noise. 'Mother said she could fix the peeling uppers with glue and the cracks in the leather would fill in nicely with a bit of blacking. She said they were leather and would last a lifetime.'

He said, 'In a way they did.'

If that was a joke it was in bad taste. 'She had the nerve to accuse me of being bossy. As I told her, I was only trying to help.'

'What did she say to that?'

'That she'd prefer the help of a gin and tonic.'

He smiled. 'I'm partial to a G and T myself.'

'It was half-past three in the afternoon.'

He cleared his throat before saying, 'They don't mean it. I expect your mother was proud of having a daughter like you.'

I drank my tea. The warm liquid would give me the strength I needed. I'd thought Mother would be easier to deal with once she was dead. 'I only wanted the best for her, as she'd always given me.' I sighed. 'To think we quarrelled over a pair of boots. If only I could chuck the wretched things in the bin.'

He stood up. 'Leave the boots with me.'

-‹‹‹•››-

The day before the service, I went to see Mother for the last time. I knew I looked tense, almost ill. I'd bought a new coat. Black doesn't suit me either. The chapel of rest was not large. I had to squeeze myself between the wall and the wooden coffin.

From half-way down, her body was draped with white lace. I didn't expect Mother to be able to still upset me. But she did. The curves of her lips were too tight, making the thin line of lipstick look as if it didn't belong on her.

'She looks lovely, doesn't she?' he asked. 'I'm pleased with the result. Old people are often tricky. Too many wrinkles to be tucked. A florid complexion. Broken veins. Your mother had a smooth skin. Takes a sweep of colour on the cheeks very nicely and enough hair to puff up bouffant style. It's a shame about the mouth. By the time I'd taken out her false teeth and stitched...'

'Stop,' I cried. 'Too much information.' I stood with my back pressed against the wall for a moment or two before bending over the body, intending to stroke Mother's hand. I felt suddenly brave enough to touch her now she was so still. But that was before my fingers touched her flesh. Sharply, I drew back my hand. I'd read about *cold as marble* but hadn't believed it.

The hand, which had been balanced finely on her hip, slipped and fell. I stared at it. Was it challenging me to pick it up, to wrap my fingers round her cold ones? I wanted to get out then, quickly, before he saw I hadn't the nerve. I wanted to run away but I couldn't. I shouldn't. It was all very well telling myself that death was the end but I had to prove to myself that I accepted it. For both our sakes.

I watched him pick up the hand and resettle it, almost touching the necklace. I had to ask. 'What have you done with her boots?'

'I've tucked them in the coffin.'

That doubt returned. He could have just thrown them into the bin. 'I'd like to see.'

He didn't take offence. 'They just fit.' Gently, he pulled back the white lace.

I stared at the black wool skirt, the two thin, bone-white legs and at the boots, settled between Mother's calves, just above her feet wearing the red court shoes. 'I wish she knew she'd still got them with her. It would make her smile.'

Turning my face away from Mother, I began to sob.

A Fish out of Water

My husband sacrificed our love to his manly pursuits in the misty, green-mud countryside. His dawn trampings in the hills left me lonely in bed. I thought early risers were early bedders. I was wrong. His evenings, and sometimes half his nights, were spent casting his fishing line in the rush of the becks. He wanted a fish, a slimy, cold-blooded creature.

They say one love drives out another. Our early passion for each other was born of the greedy physical attraction of opposites: me the cream-skinned blonde and him my swarthy mate. Our marriage was celebrated with the shared delights of eating and loving. His tongue tasted of paprika but felt slivery silver against my skin. He brought the sweet smell of fertility to our bed where he told me I tasted of caviar. We loved as we ate, with hands, mouths and noses.

I blame myself. The night before our wedding, my mother's advice to me was, 'Remember, the way to a man's heart is through his stomach.' Foolishly, I believed her. Over the years I wasted my talents on stews cooked with brown meat and soft red and orange vegetables and diverted my energies into piles of fresh clean laundry. But I was not in my element. I was a fish out of water.

My husband did try. Last summer, understanding that I was land-locked in domesticity, he booked an early holiday by the sea. It meant taking our three – aged ten, eight and five – out of school but, as I saw it, their future security was at stake. A happy mother is a happy home. My words. However, while I was enchanted by the cottage with a thatched roof and niche windows, seduced by the beer garden with baskets of lobelia and sweet pea hanging from iron fists, I was deceived by promises of togetherness.

In the early mornings, when I was amorous, our bed was empty as my husband walked the coastline. I was left to wander our children between banks of pink roses delicate enough to be sugared and eaten, along bridle paths margined by laced cow parsley and overhung with mock orange. During breezy afternoons on the beach, I paddled in the froth of the waves while the children explored rock pools. When their feet were stiff with cold, I rubbed them with towels, cleaning seaweed and sand from between their toes.

And where was my man? Dribbling his fingertips in rivers, wading through the depths, dipping his line into the soft water, waiting for a fish to rise to him, to put its lips round his bait and swallow. I waited for him to return to me, to seduce me with ruby wine, to make my body curve to his. In return I would offer him precious foods – pate de foie gras, Gravad Lax, chocolate as dark as sin.

When he appeared, having failed to catch a fish for supper, he was so emptied by his exertions that he threw himself onto our bed and slept with his eyes open. I closed them for him. He was no longer mine. I was wretched for my man with his devil fingers and their unruly invasions.

There was something else. I needed more than narrow lanes, banks of wild flowers and deserted shores. I was a woman who flowered in the sun, who loved best in the exotic.

We had honeymooned in Tuscany when, instead of visiting churches, we lay in bed until five in the afternoon, making love and a baby. Evenings were spent dining and nights wandering in the cool air. I cherished memories of fields drenched in opiates and a sea anemone floating its petals over the deep. My ears remembered the crested hoopoe calling across lemon trees. My tongue still tasted the caramelised rind of bar-b-qued porchetta. I imagined revisiting that heaven.

Before I told my family of my vision, I treated them to freshly killed lamb roasted in virgin olive oil with just a sprinkling of early thyme. Making the mint sauce, I sliced my thumb, tinting the vinegar a darker shade. When we had devoured our feast, I said, 'I have a vision for a last minute break.' I described lazy swims in the pool, long meals in trattorias and being made drunk with Chianti.

'That's all very well,' said my husband. 'What am I and the children to do?'

'There'll be pasta,' said the eldest child.

'And pizza,' said the second.

'And ice-cream,' said the youngest.

'And fishing I suppose,' conceded my husband.

In a trendy boutique I discovered two swimming costumes: one close fitting and black, transforming me into an Olympic champion; the other made of an exotic green material, softly ruched and sexily shiny. Wearing the green bathing suit and standing in front of the full-length mirror, I imagined my husband slipping his hand between the straps and spreading it…enough of that, I had packing to do.

-««•»»-

The villa sat on the edge of a ridge. Outside, the heat of molten gold burned to my bones while the pool tempted with calm ripples, as the filter hummed away unlucky insects. Inside, there were terracotta tiles, calm white walls and marble worktops. Jars of pasta quills, squiggles like children's first drawings, and fat, hollowed-out worms begged to be fed to boiling water. The salone doors opened towards the hill, curved as a woman's breasts and hips. There was a garden with a sun-dried lawn. Butterflies, attracted by the lavender, stirred the air with their softness, while the woodpecker furiously drilled holes in silver bark. Somewhere far away, grass was being cut, a dog barked and a man shouted in a deep, guttural voice. Invigorated by the purple air, I gave birth to a new strength which brought forth bravery and recklessness.

The next morning in bed, I said to my husband, 'My greatest desire is that you share this wonderland with me, to be tempted by me as much as by a fish.'

All he said was, 'If I catch a trout, will you cook it for supper?'

'I want to explore the village. Will you take the children with you?'

'They will frighten the fish. You must keep them with you.'

I studied my three youngsters. The eldest, a boy, tall for his age and with his father's dark locks, was already out on the terraces, running between the olive trees. The middle one, a girl blessed with my golden hair, was sitting on the grass, making a bouquet of dandelions and daisies, while the youngest, still small enough to behave like either sex, was naked in the plastic paddling pool, splashing hard enough to empty it.

'Look at them,' I told my husband. 'They're too happy to be dragged around old buildings.'

'They can't stay here alone.'

'This is a bewitching place. It is made for children. I am sure if they use their imagination no harm will come to them.'

'They might disappear into the valley.'

I shrugged. 'Let them.'

'How will you get them back at the end of the day?' he demanded.

'I will clap my hands three times and they will be home. That is all there is to it.'

'If you say so,' said my husband for the first time in our marriage.

Under my ribs, my heart rocked. I was free to roam.

As I left the garden, I nodded 'good-bye' to a baby moorhen in the pool. I waved to a fawn on the terraces and laughed at a white rabbit leaping across the meadow to nibble on lamb's lettuce.

The small, market town was set on the top of a hill. Keeping its seven towers in my sights, I made my way along the lane, between fields of sweet corn and up twisting paths. As I climbed higher, so did the sun. The medieval wall encircling the small town was thick, offering cool shade. I walked through one of the gates, a high, arched opening, with two giant wooden doors standing permanently open. I put my hand on one of the panels, pressing it against the ancient iron nail-heads until I held an imprint on my skin.

The short walk to the centre was cool and shaded by walls of houses, their windows watching my every step. But the sun warmed the piazza; music was coming from a church and a café had tables set out in the street. I ordered a cappuccino and biscotti and let the smooth coffee and the sweet cake lull me. I imagined my husband and I sitting at the table on the patio listening to the nightingale as the sun turned into the moon but my powers failed me and all I saw were two empty chairs.

At the sound of bells from the nearest church tower, a bridal couple stood at the top of the steps, waiting to be admired. Then, swiftly, the man turned to his new wife and pressed his mouth to her lips. He did not touch her, just fastened his kiss, giving her his promise of things to come. The crowd marked their approval with a cheer. I smiled but my heart was crying.

It was market day. The cobbled streets were thick with locals: men in blue hats gossiping on corners, women with huge baskets buying food. I admired heaps of aubergines, trays of zucchini flowers and bunches of asparagus. But the scent of oranges was killed by a strong salt smell. Turning, I found a sea food stall. Behind the counter a man wearing a blue apron was waving a long knife, its blade crested with blood. Here was an idea. Instead of waiting for my husband to catch a fish, I would buy one. How simple. I pushed away the knowledge that I had no idea of how to cook it.

'Buongiorno, bella signorina,' flattered the fishmonger. 'Che ti piace?'

What would I like?

I could not answer. His fish were unlike any I had ever seen at home. I stared at wide, flat bodies, streaked silver and brown, or at long, thick black things which must, surely, have been eels, and at masses of tiny grey prawns, not the least appetizing.

And then I saw their eyes. They stared at me, black and yellow, bright or milky-masked but all full of baleful reproach. It was as if they were saying to me, 'Eat me if you dare.'

I moved away from the counter, pushing against the full bodies of the Italian women, pressing to buy their swordfish or sea bass. I would stick to the tourists' idea of Italian food, pasta.

At one corner of the piazza was a shop hiding itself under a merry red and white striped awning. 'Burro and pasta' announced its sign. Butter and pasta. Perfect. Inside, the glass-topped cabinet displayed wide, shallow dishes of ravioli stuffed with spinach and ricotta, lasagne baked with meat balls and tiny sausage-shaped gnocchi served with sheeps' cheese. As I inhaled the mixed scents of fresh basil, saffron and pungent cheese, I vowed to win back my man. After eating anything from this emporium of delights, he would abandon fish and deny me nothing. I bought a tray of fresh lasagne, dribbling cheese sauce from its edges, and complimented the signora on her wares. I won an invitation to return the next day to watch how to stuff the delicate squares of dough. Handing me my full carrier bag, the signora told me about the bus to take me back to the villa.

My husband returned empty handed and hungry. However, eating a whole tray of pasta is not the path to erotic intimacy. After supper, we both fell into bed but only to sleep.

The next day, we rose late when the air was already hot. On the patio, I served flat salt bread with fig jam and milk shakes or coffee while I listened to my family plan their day.

'I will explore the forest,' said the eldest.

'I will search the lane for early blackberries,' said my daughter.

'I am bored with swimming,' said my baby. 'I will learn to fly.'

'I will catch a perch,' said my husband.

I kept my plans a secret.

On the way to the bus stop I heard the forest floor crackle under the feet of a muntjack, saw a hare snack on sweet petals in the lane and a wren settle on the branch of a cedar.

In the village, behind the white blinds of the pasta shop, I watched nimble fingers making fresh ravioli. The signora patted her stomach and said, 'The man, he like food, no? The food, it leads to love, yes?'

Hoping the signora was right, I spent troppo euros on fresh spaghetti, a pot of bolognaise sauce and a bottle of Tuscan virgin olive oil to be drizzled on hot white beans. Sitting in the bus, I planned an evening on the patio with citrus scented candles and purple hibiscus by each place setting. I would seduce my love into our old ways.

By midday, the pavimento around the house scorched the soles of my feet. Every creature except the crickets was silent. For my lunch I cooked penne with a rich, red tomato and pepper sauce. I scraped the spoon round the china bowl, making sure that not one little drop was wasted. I found a tub of coconut ice cream in the freezer, shivery cold after the hot pasta but so crunchy and sweet I could have eaten a second. Then I rested.

Before swimming, I unwrapped five pots of panna cotta, imagining the cooked cream and caramel topping melting on my tongue. I dawdled to the pool, taking perverse pleasure in the cut of sharp grass under my feet. The water licked my limbs and the sun kissed my shoulders. My black costume made me bold. My arms reached across the water while my legs kicked over and over. Soon, my aching neck forced my face flat against the water, and then tilted my head underneath. I discovered, to my delight, it was easier to swim below the surface than above and I breathed under water for longer and longer. I opened my eyes. Below me existed a new world of tiny spiders, diving beetles and drowning flies. Once, I spotted a thin snake, twisting and slipping through the water but when I turned to follow, it disappeared. Swallowed up by the filter perhaps. As the water enveloped my body, I found the pleasure which was missing from my life.

How I loved being in the pool on those afternoons. I twisted and turned as if the water was my lover and I was abandoning myself to his will. I became aware of my body, slithy and mimsy.

If only I could share this with my husband. I resolved to make more effort. I must reclaim him for myself or my life would be as nothing. That evening, I would offer him not a meal we could eat at home but neither cold, flabby fish. I would prepare an epicurean sea food dish. That meant another trip into town but I promised myself it would be worth the effort.

Later, before my shower, I studied myself in the full-length mirror. All that pasta was having an effect. My black costume was becoming tight. It stretched across my stomach, my breasts pushed out of the cups. Voluptuous might be the word. I liked my new self, my fuller shape. I prayed my husband would too.

When the sun slipped and the shadows of the olive trees grew longer on the terraces, I clapped my hands three times and watched, gratified, as the muntjack trotted up the lane. Then the hare hopped across the lawn and the wren took a dust bath under an oleander bush.

My husband arrived home when the skies were filled with wisps of fairy pinks and blues. I watched as he set his rod by the door. He shrugged off his poacher's jacket and tugged at the feet of the waders until they fell with a squelch onto the grass. I tiptoed over to him. I could smell the watercress on his feet and reached up to touch his weathered cheeks. I kissed him on the lips.

'What's that for?' he said. 'I'm knackered and starving. And before you ask, no I didn't catch a fish.'

That night I cooked spaghetti alle vongole but, as well as white clams, I added blue mussels, black cuttle fish, red snapper, yellow baby octopus and pink prawns. The children ate with relish and their fingers, picking fishy bits out of the sauce.

They told us stories of their day. The smallest one said he had learnt to sky-dive from the highest branch. He had been attacked by a buzzard but the curved beak snapped empty and he dropped softly onto a bed of dry pine needles. Our daughter recounted how she had met a wild tortoise. They had agreed not to race but to wander slowly up the lane, nibbling at each new plant they met, later comparing flavours. She said the experiment was going well until a car ran over the tortoise, who could not reach the ditch quickly enough. Our eldest son described galloping through the forest until he reached a clearing. He was nosing among the grass when he heard a dog bark. As he lifted his head, a shot from a gun singed his ear. Luckily, the hunter was slow in re-loading and the boy skipped quickly among the chestnut trees.

When the children were in bed, my husband, said, 'You are putting our children in danger. Our son might have been carted away dead on a pole and our daughter could have been killed by that car. As for our littlest one, like a new-born lamb, he was at the mercy of a predator. I insist you stop at home and look after them.'

I argued with him. 'They are having adventures. Don't put them behind bars. That is not love. Let them be free, free to grow. Have you no soul?'

As I undressed for the night, I heard him, in the spare room, curse me as he spread sheets and stuffed a pillow case.

Alone in the huge matrimonial bed I flexed my limbs across the mattress and tried whispering my fingers on skin, around the fullness of my thighs and, finally, to the parting in my body. But as I touched inside, I felt no warm tremoring flesh, just an arid, empty space. I lay, too much awake, between the sheets, angry with myself for failing to arouse my husband until, eventually, sleep came into the window with the moths and stayed until the far hills turned deep violet. Later, the moon brought in her own blue temperature and at dawn I heard the rain. When we went outside for breakfast, the garden was a glory of azure chicory, newly opened against the wet grass.

My husband announced to the children that he was taking them fishing. 'Your mother will not care for you. Therefore the task is mine. I feel lucky. Today we will catch a fish.'

'I will be a shark,' said the eldest son, 'and catch a fish first.'

'I will be a mermaid,' said the girl, 'and sit on a rock while I comb my hair.'

'I will be a tiddler,' said the little one, 'and swim in the warm shallows.'

'You will do as you're told,' said their father, 'and help me.'

I changed to the green swimsuit. My body filled it gloriously, the fabric puckering, layered like scales. In the mirror, I saw that my cheeks were rounder. My jaw line was softened, and blended into my neck, which sloped into my shoulders. I ran a hand over my abdomen. It was abundant. Too lazy to exert myself, I floated on my back, occasionally rescuing a ladybird from drowning. Later, I prepared rotolo di spinaci, with delicately thin dough and a purée of spinach, egg and cheese.

That evening, my blue necklace sat well on my still damp skin, the beads shining softly as eyes beneath the sea. Putting on my earrings, I discovered that my ears had soft, frilly edges, no doubt softened by the water. I hung them with pearl drops.

My hair had grown down my back. I pushed it into heavy ripples, turning to see the effect in the mirror. I longed for the return of my husband and the loving which surely must follow supper.

Eventually stones crunched under the wheels of the car.

I heard the youngest child shriek, 'Mummy, guess what? Daddy caught a fish.'

Rotolo doesn't keep. The proof of my devotion went into the bin. Knocking back pinot grigio, I glared at my husband as he slit the fish open, gutted it and cooked it in white wine. I both admired that fish which had won my husband's attention and hated it.

I slept heavily and when I went down to the kitchen in the morning, the four of them had left. For another successful day, no doubt.

I decided not to shop or cook. If I could not please my husband, I'd spend the hours pleasing myself. I spent the morning reading a romantic novel in which the heroine did exactly what the hero demanded and found everlasting happiness.

'I will make you mine,' said the hero. 'You will want for nothing.'

'My master,' said the heroine. 'I will obey your every wish.'

'Pfft,' I thought. 'I'll find happiness, but I'll do it my way.'

Since I couldn't be defeated by a fish, I would do whatever it took. I was as good, no, better, than any creature which came out of the water.

That afternoon, I felt born to swim. My bulk was light in the water, in its true element, it skimmed up and down. My arms lay flat against my body, my hands flapping. My legs were one, my feet moving together, a gentle paddle that guided me through the water. I blew bubbles up towards the sun. When, eventually, I broke the surface, I found it impossible to breathe so I dived again. My hair flowed and spread about me, silver seaweed. I laughed at the spiders caught at the bottom and even at a snake trying to skate up the wall of the pool. My lips opened and closed, and I did not drown. My mouth widened only to snap at a flailing ladybird. She tasted sweet. I knew now I didn't need men or children. I would stay here, in the pool, under the sparkling water, gliding, turning and diving. My eyes saw a thousand flickering lights, my tail paddled and my fins flapped. I was complete. Almost.

When I heard a car drive up the lane, I lay still, just under the surface, and waited. My husband slammed the door. His voice was loud and angry. He had no fish to eat. Fuzzily, as if they were a long way away, the children called me.

'Mummy, I tried to catch a fish and be a man.'

'Mummy, I tried to kiss a frog but it hopped away.'

'Mummy, where are you?'

Footsteps ran along the pavimento and across the grass.

'Daddy, quickly. In the pool.'

A shadow hung over the deep. I swam quickly but the

shadow kept up. A hook dangled before me, baited with a prawn smeared with cream. I tried to twist away but the moist, pink morsel was more than I could resist. I felt the prawn in my mouth, then a sudden sharpness. The line pulled, I tugged. Pain seared. I tasted blood.

As the water drained from under me, I twirled in the air and gasped. The heat threatened to dry my scales to the death.

'Isn't it great, Daddy?'

'Where did it come from, Daddy?'

'Take it back to the house, Daddy.'

'Supper.' His voice was triumphant. 'Back to the villa.'

He led and the children marched behind. They made a procession of pagans, bearing their victim to the altar. Slurp and I was in the kitchen sink, thrashing against the porcelain. Twist and thrash, and I was spread upon warm wood.

I opened my mouth but no words came.

'Look, Daddy. It's trying to speak to us.'

'Don't be daft, that's just what they do.'

'I don't like it, Daddy.'

'It's just a fish.' My hunter put his knife to my throat. When it pricked me, my blood welled a rose. I made one last effort and rolled my eyes at my offspring.

The smell is intoxicating. Melting butter, bubbling white wine, bay leaves and crushed parsley.

How can I attract his attention? I must. It isn't too late. We can still be together.

Lying on the chopping board, I have a revelation, realise what's missing in the pool. It's cold in the water. Cold and lonely. There's no touch, no love.

My husband lifts me out of the pan. He slips me onto a plate. He is going to eat me. The children can't help me, they are too innocent. Even my eldest son can't understand but has abandoned me to his father's will. We are alone. He is to eat me all by himself. A greedy man. He sits down at the table and picks up his knife and fork.

At the first cut, I shiver. As he raises a portion of me to his lips, the shiver becomes a tremble. My excitement grows. I am going into his mouth. I will learn what no woman has ever discovered, what it is to enter a man.

His mouth is soft around me, his teeth merely a scratch. I am not frightened. As he loves the taste of me, I love slipping into his warm depths. Yet, when he puts the final slice of me into him I open my mouth to cry out as, with one huge convulsion, I slip out of this world and away.

Blood Red Berries

I disliked Barbara Conrad the minute I took notice of her.

I was still in my 'anger' stage, so I can hardly lay all the blame at her feet, but it amused me to do so and I needed some entertaining. My wife had died two months previously and I had taken it hard. If you want to know the truth, I resented her leaving me. I was only fifty-five, too young to be a widower and, while she had been a year older, it didn't seem fair that she was torn away from me by a wretched woman's disease. Her death left me bereft. We had no children and my only brother ran a logging company in Brazil.

Taking advice from the doctor, whose unfortunate duty it was to inform me that my wife had breathed her last, I attended classes on 'the grieving process.' The word *process* made me feel like a sausage rolling off the production line and I believed none of it, except, yes, I was angry.

I was idling on my laptop one afternoon. Machines can't say things like *Anger is a recognised phase of the mourning process* or *work your way towards moving on* and I was content to browse through the invitations to join so-and-so on *Facebook* or *Linked In*. My attention was drawn to a travel company selling cruises. Being shut up on a ship with hundreds of strangers was not my idea of a holiday and, although my wife had tentatively suggested one, I'd resisted. But if I'd wanted an excuse to change my mind, the prospect of a female Prime Minister was enough to drive me overseas.

The advice to *enjoy exceptional value* and *visit the beautiful and vibrant green island of…* encouraged me. Whether a cruise was a way of escaping, or the acceptable moving on, didn't bother me. The open sea with promises of new sights and sounds appealed and when I discovered the ship had a scheduled stop in Brazil, I picked up the telephone and dialled.

'Certainly,' said the voice laced with syrup. 'We have openings for that cruise.'

The minute we'd agreed that a standard cabin midships would suit me, the voice suggested I upgrade to the deck above.

'You wouldn't be wanting a suite, sir, not as a single passenger, but this cabin has a bath as well as a shower and a mini-bar.' She paused before she enticed me with, 'it's the last available one on this superior level.'

The only disadvantage hinted at was that I might have to share a table at mealtimes, but any doubts I had were swiftly cancelled by the anticipation of island hopping in the West Indies, via a visit to my brother. I packed, eager for the congenial surroundings, good food and, who knew, the company of an elegant lady if I cared for after-dinner dancing.

-◄◄◄◆►►►-

A chauffeur driven limousine carried me to the Southampton docks. Once on board, my cabin, with its settee, desk and dolls' house refrigerator, pleased me, although the bachelor's single bed reminded me of my careless wife. The afternoon passed with unpacking, exploring the ship, buying a bottle of gin and dressing for dinner. The dress code for the first night was *smart casual*. I clothed myself with the kind of garments in which I was naturally comfortable, matching the velvet jacket with a silk cravat.

The dining hall of the Isabella was vast with chairs upholstered in pink velvet. I asked for a single table.

The Maître D' sported oily hair and a smile to match. 'There is no available small table but Mr and Mrs Conrad are very pleasant. You will like them, you'll see.'

I told myself that the name 'Conrad' added a literary air to my adventure.

Until I followed him across the room towards a table with a couple already seated. The man looked harmless enough, slight with a snub nose and a pair of spectacle frames the same shade of grey as his suit. He gave me a meek smile and half rose. I waved him down and turned to his wife, a large woman with a face the colour of a good port, her lipstick quarrelling with her complexion. She nodded to me as if I were her lap dog begging for permission to join her.

That was the point at which I took a dislike to her. Perhaps I was being over sensitive. I managed a 'Good evening.'

'Barbara,' she said.

I sat opposite Mr Conrad, who told me, 'I'm Jonathan but everyone calls me Johnnie.'

I said my name was Edward Bishop and I preferred not to be called either Ed or Eddie.

The moment we opened our menus, Barbara leaned across to me. 'You want to have the beef. The beef is excellent on this ship. It's not so good on their river cruises but on this one it's delicious. Isn't it Johnnie?'

Another one of those pale smiles.

I studied the menu.

'I wouldn't have the soup.' Her perfume was sweet and suffocating like an orchard refusing to fruit. 'The appetisers are good but the soup can be rather heavy. Take the beef.'

I put down my menu. 'Maybe I'll go to the buffet.'

'You can't.' Her voice was triumphant. 'Not in the evenings. Just tell the waiter how you like your beef.'

I summoned the waiter. 'The citrus cocktail, the tomato soup and the sole.' I paused. 'And the wine list.'

'We usually have one white and one red. If you don't drink the whole bottle, they'll keep it for you, won't they Johnnie?'

Johnnie cleared his throat as if he was going to make a comment but had decided against it.

'You've chosen the very best company to cruise with. We've enjoyed many cruises but the best have always been on this ship.'

When I told them this was my first, Barbara twinkled at me. 'A cruise virgin. How sweet.'

It was unforgivably rude of me but my response was, 'I'm here to recover from my wife's death.'

This statement had a rapid effect on Johnnie, who coloured and grinned at me. 'What better way to tidy up such an experience but to have fun.'

Barbara put a hand on her husband's arm. 'Edward might not share your sense of humour, dear.'

I remained silent.

The food was tolerable. I had only to eat and listen. Barbara declaimed on holidays and cruise companies, her monologue including many 'I know all about...' and 'We've always had the best, haven't we Johnnie?' She made great play of the fact that they were in a suite on the deck above mine and that one of the advantages was they could breakfast in their room.

I drank steadily through my bottle of Sancerre, promising myself a solitary egg and bacon for my breakfast.

After the ice cream and chocolate mousse, declining coffee, I said 'Good night.'

Barbara twiddled her fingers at me, four chubby puppets. 'No doubt we shall be seeing you at the show.'

'Show?'

She beamed. 'The very best. There's a comedian and a crooner who's on the TV. Well-known names.'

Informing her I didn't watch the television apart from the news and shows were not to my taste, I left them to their petit fours.

At eight o'clock the following morning I visited the Garden Café and ate in complete silence.

Our first port of call was to be the Cape Verde Islands. After reading the pre-port information sheets left in my cabin, I booked myself onto a walking tour and looked forward to the fresh air and exercise. However, after eating dinner, when a good Burgundy had loosened my tongue, I foolishly shared my choice with Barbara and Johnnie.

The bosom heaved. 'You've made quite the wrong choice. We've opted for the coach tour, haven't we Johnnie?'

'You don't walk?' I enquired of Johnnie.

He shrugged. 'Barbara always chooses the tours. She...'

'I expect your wife made all the arrangements for you.' Barbara patted my hand, which I'd left idling on the table. 'Perhaps you'd appreciate my help, Eddie?'

I had a fleeting memory of my wife and I pouring over a map laid out on the dining table, me reading from the guide book and my wife busily scribbling notes in an old shorthand notebook. I allowed myself a silent cry of regret and gave 'Babs' a look of pure contempt.

Which she ignored. 'If I change our tour to yours, I can point out places of interest and we'd have coffee together.'

The woman was wearing a dress patterned with purple and yellow roses, but I don't think that was why I felt the need to excuse myself and flee. As I pushed back my chair, she said, 'I hope you've packed sturdy shoes. Trails abroad are always filthy.'

-◄◄◄◆▶▶▶-

The ship's engines were quiet. Before I turned in, I took a stroll around the deck. The sea was a sheet of dark cloth embroidered with silver, the lights from land sparkling messages of promise. I felt strangely uplifted and found the courage to counsel myself. I had loved my wife dearly but I wouldn't have wanted her to suffer any more than she did. Cruel fate had offered me the chance of a second life and I should take it.

-◄◄◄◆▶▶▶-

Next morning I joined my group on the quayside to stare at men scrubbing fishing boats, women selling the early morning's catch and stallholders expecting passengers to waste their money on souvenirs.

We were about to board the coach taking us to higher ground, when I saw Barbara trotting towards me, followed by Johnnie. Both were wearing laced boots and those canvas hats with corks round the brim. It was a warm, dry day and my soft suede shoes and light denim jacket were perfectly suitable. I carried a shooting bag housing a pair of binoculars and a bottle of water from my refrigerator and I held my trusty walking stick. I was relaxed, enjoying my new life, but at the sight of my new friends I cursed the devil and all his demons.

Barbara's skin was a worrying shade of fuchsia. 'Eddie, thank heavens we've caught up with you. I said to Johnnie, that poor man. He'll have no idea of what's in store, the unhygienic comfort stops and the boys selling junk by the side of the road. He'll need my help.'

I forced a smile. 'That's most thoughtful of you but I was looking forward to exploring solo.'

Which made Johnnie laugh. 'No hope, old boy, no hope at all.' He added, 'Quite a thought, being single again.'

On the coach, I slipped into the last seat at the back. The Conrads settled in front of me. Barbara began by advising me on 'the route and the very best views' but, after about five minutes, the effort of twisting her thick torso proved too much for her and she contained herself to pointing out to her husband the 'lazy and disgusting ways' of 'people who lived abroad'. He kept quiet, staring out of the window with his nose more or less pressed against the glass in spite of his wife's assurances that 'these coaches are always filthy.'

Half an hour later, we embarked on a pleasant walk with stunning views of the bay. The Conrads kept to the back. 'Just to make sure we don't lose anyone,' Barbara trilled.

At one point, the guide stopped to point out a short plant with a thick yellow stem and berries as red as fresh blood. 'Many poisonous plants on island. These berries bitter. The juice makes men sick. And kills.'

I heard Johnnie titter. Not laugh but titter, that *I'm trying to be discreet but this got the better of me* underhand noise.

Barbara turned to him. 'I don't see anything funny in poison.'

Johnnie cleared his throat. 'Of course not dear.'

I made a feeble attempt to break the tension. 'At least we won't be picking it.'

We stared at the offensive plant as if we needed to know not to dip it in batter and fry it.

As we continued our way, Barbara was beside me. 'He's very good, our guide.'

I agreed with her.

'It's usual to tip at the end of the tour. If you don't have change, Johnnie will lend it to you.'

I assured her I had the necessary small coins.

She stopped and turned round. 'Where on earth has Johnny got to? Poor man has a weak heart.'

He wasn't far behind so I called, 'Come along, old chap, we'll miss coffee.'

Barbara gave me a furious look. 'No one has ever called my husband 'old chap'.

I shrugged. 'There's a first time for everything.'

-«««◆»»»-

The restaurant where we were to eat lunch was one of those garish establishments with a terrace elaborately fenced with bamboo swirls and loops and, on the floor, red tiles echoing each click of the waiters' heels. Pandering to the supposed wishes of tourists, the tables were open to the sky.

The walk had given me an appetite and I could sleep off any wine later as the ship prepared to leave port. 'Care to share a bottle of rose?' I asked Johnnie.

The sun rose. The heat increased. Barbara's hat did nothing to protect the back of her neck and try as Johnnie did, he could not dilute her discomfort as her skin burned and her cheeks glistened with sweat.

His manner towards her was almost too tender. 'I am sorry, my sweetie.' He reached across the table and took her hand. 'As soon as we are back on board, you must lie down.'

I almost sniggered but was saved by the tortured manner in which Barbara poured herself a glass of water.

When we returned to the dockside, I paused at a stall offering objects carved from various woods. Once we reached Brazil, I planned to hop off the boat to visit my brother up river. I chose a sheathed paper knife as a suitable gift for him. My purchase seemed to revive Barbara, who bought a lidded box decorated with carved flowers and leaves, commenting, 'I have no idea what I shall keep inside but I'm sure it will come in useful.'

However, back on the ship, she retired to her cabin, escorted by Johnnie muttering, 'I'll make you one of those green teas you are fond of.'

As we drew into deep waters, Johnnie joined me on deck. 'Barbara's not up to much. I've told her to stay put.' He nudged me, actually dug his elbow into my side. 'We can have a bit of fun at dinner.' He had a sly grin on his face. 'Fancy working our way through the wine list? You know the kind of thing. Aperitif, white wine with the soup…?'

'Sherry,' I corrected him.

He raised his eyebrows. 'If you say so, old boy. Sort of thing you'd know.'

Gratified that he acknowledged my superiority in one realm, I happily followed his lead. 'A Sancerre with the fish, Burgundy with the meat, Beaujolais with the cheese and Sauterne with the desert.'

'A cognac in the bar afterwards?'

'We're at sea for three days. What else is there to do but eat and drink?'

Although I felt bad for Barbara, I was attracted to the idea of just the two of us 'having fun'.

-««•»»-

During the time it took to cross the Atlantic, I didn't see poor Barbara, as I came to think of her. Johnnie told me she had developed severe sickness and a fever.

'What on earth caused that?' I asked.

34

'I wish I knew. All I'm doing is helping her sip those disgusting green teas she favours.'

While we were at sea, Johnnie left me to my games of bridge and constitutionals around deck until we met at dinner when we continued in our game of wine tasting. In which Johnnie delighted. You'd never guess he had a wife languishing in her cabin.

'How's Barbara?' I asked each evening.

His reply only varied in the vocabulary. Barbara was 'making the most of a bad job' or was 'totally fed up with the whole ghastly business' or was 'sick as an almost dead carthorse, old boy' and he was 'feeling dreadful on her account' but could only 'keep up with the green tea.'

'Have you consulted the ship's doctor?'

'Never had much time for them. If you want my honest opinion I think they're nothing but a load of skivers, enjoying a free break while their colleagues work all the hours in our hospitals.'

The prejudice of the man appalled me. I was reminded of my initial dislike for the couple and looked forward to arriving in the jungles of Brazil.

We were making good progress with the intention of docking at Santarem in a couple of days. On a whim, I ordered a bottle of champagne. A gesture which proved to be totally inappropriate. Johnnie arrived in the dining room wearing an expression of despondency.

I adopted a jocular tone in the hope it would cheer him up. 'What's the matter, old boy?'

He sat down. 'It's Barbara. The doc says she must be hospitalised or there's no hope for her.'

'That bad?'

He nodded and, pulling out a handkerchief, blew his nose. 'He still doesn't know what's causing it but he does know he can't help her.'

'What's the plan? You take her off the ship at Santarem?'

'Can't wait. They're going to airlift her this evening.' He glanced at his watch. 'About now. Want to watch?'

Not sure on the etiquette for this bizarre situation, I followed him up on deck. Above the stern of the ship, a helicopter circled making that clackety racket. We walked along the deck only to find our way barred by a red and white striped rope. We watched as a rope ladder was thrown from the 'copter' to be caught by a member of crew. By leaning over the rail we could see a stretcher being fixed to the bottom rungs of the ladder. On the stretcher was a body well wrapped in blankets.

I glanced at Johnnie who was watching the proceedings with a calmer expression on his face than I'd manage if that were my wife. The poor woman was hauled up to disappear into the helicopter, which then swung round and flew away.

I stood and waited.

Johnnie seemed transfixed.

'She'll be OK, old chap.' I gave him a gentle slap on the back. 'They'll have hospitals as good as those at home.'

That roused him. He turned to me and winked. 'I was wondering about joining the bridge set after dinner. After all, no need to rush back to my cabin anymore.'

The following day, as we approached land, we experienced a happening which seemed little short of a miracle. The weather had been getting warmer for the last few days and as Johnnie had no need to stay in his cabin, we took a turn around the deck. Which was invaded by a mass of butterflies, literally hundreds of them, flying here and there, settling on the rail or the window frames, now and again even settling on us, on our shoulders or bare arms. It was the nearest I'd ever come to magic and it was a truly extraordinary scene, with these blue and yellow creatures surrounding us.

It took Johnnie's mind off his sick wife and entertained the two of us as we approached the shore. Where we took our leave of each other, Johnnie to travel to the hospital where his wife was waiting for him and me to my brother's plantation.

We shook hands. 'I hope, by the time we meet again, your wife will be her old self.'

Johnnie, returned to his formal gloomy self, shook his head. 'We can only hope for the best.'

-·«‹◆›»·-

I was surprisingly glad to see my brother, who looked well if weathered. That evening, to my amusement, we changed into slacks and a jacket since, according to my brother, 'My man prefers it and at least the mosquitoes won't get us.'

His 'man' was a more than adequate cook and we indulged ourselves, unimpeded by the advantage of a woman's presence. My brother told me he'd arranged a couple of days off from the factory and suggested that the next day we visit the logging works.

'So you can see what I get up to,' he promised.

The drive was not a long one and we spent all day at the logging works, where I marvelled at the great piles of tree trunks and learned how they were transformed into huge logs to be transported around the world. Lunch, taken at a local café, was simple but fortifying and in the afternoon we drove through the jungle, where my brother pointed out a great, green snake. It was hanging in a tree immediately above us. We were in an open-topped Land Rover. Instinctively I ducked.

My brother laughed. 'It's not poisonous. You're quite safe. Lives on lizards and frogs. But it is a boa.'

I gazed at the emerald body wrapped around the branch, beautiful in its way, with diamond shaped markings and a brilliant yellow belly. But I still shuddered.

I was happy to agree to the plan that we do more sightseeing the next day but, as we were about to depart, he had a telephone call requiring he be back at the factory sooner than expected. I enjoyed a quiet day, sitting on the low balcony at the back of his house, reading and recording events in my journal. While I was gazing into the undergrowth on the far side of the balcony rail, something attracted my attention with a scrabbly snuffly noise. I got up and leaned over the rail and, to my delight, saw a porcupine shovelling old and new leaves aside, making faster progress than I'd imagined. I watched him until he disappeared under the dross of the jungle floor. As I understood these creatures were normally nocturnal, I felt I'd had a bit of luck.

That evening I told my story to my brother.

'Oh, he's often about. Seems a sweet natured thing.'

Deflated that I hadn't made a great discovery, I moved on to describe my travelling companions.

His response gratified me. 'Sound a couple of absolute horrors. Why go back on board? Stay with me for as long as you want and then fly home.'

The offer was tempting but I felt a strange desire to join Johnnie again. I know it sounds ridiculous, but I had the sensation he needed me.

-«««•»»»-

Which proved to be the case.

My brother kindly drove me to the port of Manaus, where I was to re-join the Isabella. Bidding him 'Goodbye and thank you', I made for the Garden Café, where I found Johnnie sitting by himself, sipping a broth, looking as if he had lost his entire world.

Settling myself on a chair I said, 'You look pretty down.'

He pulled out his handkerchief which looked as if it were more than a day old. He dabbed at his eyes. 'It's Barbara.'

A fear filled me as strange as that earlier idea of mine that I had to get back to the ship. 'What about her?'

'She's dead.'

My adrenalin ran. 'Dead? How?'

'That's just it, old boy. No one knows.'

'Who doesn't know?'

'Me. The hospital doctor. The Maitre D' here.'

'What the hell has he got to do with it?'

'The food, old man.' He shrugged. 'Not one single person on the ship has been taken ill. Only my beloved Barbara.'

We were at a table for two but it was as if there was an extra chair upholstered in pink and purple. Empty.

I did a most uncharacteristic thing. I reached my hand across the table. When Johnnie took it, I felt a fool.

'She breathed her last yesterday morning. As the sun rose.' He gave a great sob.

I sensed we were being watched, twisted my hand free and asked what happened next.

'I didn't want to lose her.'

I hadn't wanted to lose my wife but my life had more than picked up since.

He hadn't noticed my silence. 'I arranged her cremation.'

'You mean…?'

'Keep her with me. The Captain said he had no objection to my bringing her ashes on board.' He allowed himself a smile. 'After all, I had the urn.' He reached behind his back for the box which his wife had bought from that stallholder and put it on the table.

I stared at it. The innocent wooden artefact had suddenly taken on a dark complexion.

'It's obvious. Ideal in fact.' His laugh reverberated around the room. 'Just like Barbara to provide for her future.'

-◄◄◄◆►►►-

That evening we left Manaus and began the journey home. I drank my gin and tonic in my cabin before making my way to the dining room, thinking that even though Johnnie was on board, he wouldn't want a public appearance. I was expecting to eat alone. But there he was and not alone. On the table was the box.

He grinned at me and nodded towards it. 'Didn't think you'd mind, old chap. Sure you'd want her too, just as I do.'

Johnnie was transformed. Both for the good and the not so good. He kept up a string of amusing banter about his time in Manaus, pretty much making fun of the place and people.

'While Barbara was cooking, I took a boat inland, up river. The locals thought me mad. Said the youngster's rowing was untrustworthy and the boat would leak.'

'He wasn't?'

'Course not. All great fun.' Then he winked at me. 'Just the kind of thing Barbara would have poured cold water on. Most enjoyable.' He glanced at the box. 'Wonder if she's happy in there? Should be. It was her choice.'

I managed to eat the food, all except the vanilla mousse sprinkled with drifts of poppy seeds. I'd never seen anyone's ashes but I suspected they were fine and dusky coloured.

Over coffee, he said, 'What d'you think of this then, old chap?'

'What's that?'

'We're now two crusty old bachelors, right? Suppose we joined forces for the odd cruise or two? You know the kind of thing. Stay at home on our own until we feel the need to get out and about, and then take a holiday together. Separate cabins, of course. What d'you say?'

I didn't have anything to say, it was too much of a surprise. I had expected any man, sitting with his wife's ashes on the table, possibly still warm, to be at least reticent about making immediate plans. Clearly I was wrong because he nodded towards the relics and added, 'Barbara would come too.'

It occurred to me that it could be amusing: a couple of men travelling the world by ship, meeting when it suited them, enjoying the privacy of their own cabins when it didn't. Still, I needed time to consider.

As if sensing this, Johnnie drained his coffee cup, pushed back his chair and stood up. 'No rush. We've the whole of the Atlantic to make plans. But it's a good idea. Until we find each other trying, of course.' He smiled as if he had an idea up his sleeve. And he took his leave.

As I was pondering what on earth would make a man consider travelling with another man if he thought there was the slightest possibility the two of them might find each other trying, I noticed Johnnie had left behind his miniature coffin. There it sat, on the table. I came to the conclusion it might be wise if this scheme of Johnnie's started with a short trip around the Mediterranean.

Pleased I had taken a decision, I considered the box. A pretty little thing. With such a ghoulish cargo. Not that I had seen human ashes before. My good wife had a respectable burial in the family plot. I had the chance of adding to my life experiences. I glanced round the dining room. It was empty apart from a young couple holding hands and whispering. Did I feel guilty? Not really. Johnnie would never know. What harm could one quick peep do?

I reached out, drew the box closer, and gently lifted the lid. I looked. Adrenalin ran through my veins. Ashes certainly, grey and crumbly soft. And two shrivelled blood red berries.

The Assumption

Je m'appelle Hélène Salomé. A Noël passé, j'ai donné un baiser d'adieu à mon mari.

Under my lips his forehead was chilly but smooth as though he was untroubled. I shuddered. He had not changed then, even in death. Resigned, I pulled myself upright and swept my fingers over his eyes to close them. I could not cry although I did love him, once, when we were both young and innocent. Too innocent some might say for Henri had not the dreams of a silly girl who longed for the passion and hot kisses of the paperback romances. On our wedding night he claimed me in silence, his vow, made in church to worship me with his body, apparently forgotten. Pleasure, I discovered too late, was not a word in his vocabulary.

What had I expected? I came, like many French girls of my time, from a Catholic family. I was not, nor ever had been, a good Catholic girl. Without believing or doubting, I received the Blessed Sacrament from a young age, ignoring the statue of the Virgin appraising me as I left church after the Mass. Maybe like many French girls, I avoided examining the other statue, the one of Our Lord, his carved body hanging on the cross, his flesh torn and bleeding in sacrificial love.

My adoration I gave to a tiny, gold painted angel which lived in a niche in the church wall by the font. As soon as I could walk, I snatched my hand from my mother's grasp, left her with her women friends, and ran to talk to my angel.

'*Bonjour,*' I would say. '*Je m'appelle Hélène. Je suis bien contente de te rencontrer. S'il te plaît, veux tu être mon ami?*

It was not until I had grown from childhood that I accepted that the angel's smile had been put there by the sculptor.

Soon my head was full of dreams of another kind of love, of courtship and marriage with its intimate knowledge which came with that secret act between man and wife.

-◄◄◄◆►►►-

Henri arrived in Anché amidst a gaggle of gossip. On the corners of the lanes, the women exchanged news.

'At last the empty shop on the high street has been leased.'

'The new owner is a butcher.'

'But we have a butcher. Do we need two?'

'Not my problem. I will buy my meat where I always do. From the market.'

'He must already be a man of substance,' said the wife of the notaire. 'He has also bought that empty property opposite the church. It'll need some restoration to make it a comfortable home.'

The gossips insisted he had come to our village to find a wife, but I decided he was part of the wave of re-growth taking place all over Europe since the end of hostilities with the Germans. We all expected great things from our new life in the 1950s.

Before the owner of the business arrived in the village, came the renovators. The shop was stripped of the ancient wooden interior. Out came the minute windows with their square panes and in went a huge piece of plate glass. Behind it were established two display shelves covered with red cloths.

'That's to make the meat look bright and fresh,' said one woman.

Out came the old polished counter, half-eaten with worm, to lie in the street. In went a white and green marbled slab inserted with a wooden board on which to chop the meat. Finally, up went a spanking new blind, red and white striped, and outside the shop stood a board announcing,

OPENING SOON
AN EMPORIUM OF PORK, LAMB, BEEF
HOMEMADE SAUSAGES AND PIES

The new member of our community was not tall but he had a broad chest, a well-cut beard and a head of thick, black hair.

I developed an interest in shopping and preparing the simple evening meal for myself and my parents. I bought sausages both plain and spicy and several different types of pie. I left the sausages for my mother who retained her authority over our hot midday meal but I took a delight in laying out one of the pies with a green salad and a bowl of tomatoes for our final *repas*. Both the sausages and the pies were rich with the tang of good meat, salt and black pepper. The added spice in some varieties did not offend my father's digestion. My mother, as her neighbours did, abandoned our usual butcher and joined the queue outside the new establishment.

Henri had a habit of winking at me as he handed me my change and I felt myself blushing. Of course he attended Mass on Sunday mornings but also during the week. One Monday, early in the day after I had been to buy fresh baguettes from the *boulangerie*, he fell in with me and walked with me until we reached my parents' house at the far end of the village. After that, he escorted me home each Sunday, always making his stride long enough to keep us a little ahead of my mother and father. His comments on the gardens we passed, the displays in the windows of the few shops we had along the main street and the progress on his new home made for entertaining listening.

He told me his house was built on land which was once an orchard so he was naming it *Le Verger*. He was always polite, bidding *Au revoir* to both me and my parents at our gate. So when he invited me to accompany him to a recital in the *centre communautaire*, I accepted.

It turned out we both had a taste for Fauré. The cool beauty of the music made me cry and he offered me a spotlessly white handkerchief with which to wipe away my tears. That night, as he said, 'Au revoir', he gave me a timid kiss on the cheek.

The following spring, after a Sunday service, he offered me an Easter wedding.

I married Henri out of a certain knowledge that he was the best husband I was likely to find in a small village in a remote part of my country.

My joy was transitory. He might have loved me in his way but his duty was to his butchering. His customers grew steadily in number and the only other butcher in the village closed his shop. He worked hard; that I couldn't complain about.

But his priorities left me lonely. Each morning when I woke, restored by sleep, the warm blood ran quickly in my veins and an urgency deep in my body made me turn at once to the other side of the bed. It was empty, the sheets already cold. For my husband had left me alone and was already kneeling at the early Mass to meet his longing for holy blessings, even on those days when he had to travel to another village to find a priest. All I had of him was the dip on the pillow left by his head. At night he joined me in our bed after he had said his prayers and when it was pitch dark. Henri treated me as part of his home, expecting me to do my duty as a housewife as he did his as a husband. His passion he reserved for the Virgin Mary.

-«««•»»»-

After a year of marriage, I gave birth to a boy. Henri was delighted, calling him his 'little angel'. He carved him a cradle out of a huge chestnut trunk and, the minute the child cried to be suckled, he called, 'Hélène, you are wanted.'

How I wished those words meant something lustier, but Henri did not believe in indulging himself. I could not complain, since the child gave me a feeling of fulfilment which was not granted to me in our bed. Becoming a mother brought the ecstasy I desired.

We christened him Gabriel and he thrived. On Sunday mornings, in gratitude, I swaddled him to my body so that I might receive the sacrament. Each week, as Gabriel grew, my love blossomed and I crossed myself before Our Lady. I flattered myself that at last we shared a common emotion, that holy bond between mother and son. I was deluded.

Before the year was out, Gabriel's peach-soft face had shrunk to a blue moon; his skin stretched across his bones. As daily I prayed, daily he suffered; his breathing rasping in his chest, his little fingers clenching the air, failing the strength to cling to my breast.

Henri did his best. He spent his savings on visits from the doctor; he purchased milk-fed veal to make broth for the boy and he lit a new candle every day before Mass. I continued my habit of taking Gabriel to church, but his body, bandaged to my chest, grew lighter and more fragile. I interceded for him but the Virgin smiled coldly on us and did not share her grace with us. She rejected my pleas. At the turn of the year, my son journeyed to heaven and I was, once more, alone with my husband.

Then I cried.

For my baby's tiny grave, I asked the stone mason to carve a miniature angel and every day I visited this angel pleading with him to look after my child. And stayed away from the Mass. The Virgin might flex plaster lips but that smile was wasted on me. I felt nothing for Her but envy. She had enjoyed the company of Her Son for thirty years, while I had been allowed a mean twelve months. We no longer shared a bond and my love for religion shrivelled as my Gabriel's body had shrivelled.

'Come to Mass,' Henri begged. 'I am afraid for your soul.'

'Pfft,' I said. 'I will take care of my soul. You look to your duties to Mother Church.'

-«««◆»»»-

The years passed, following their seasons as I followed mine. My husband assumed my passions were spent, leaving me with nothing but to provide for the table and my store cupboard. Gardening, planting cabbages among the wild flowers and beans against the fence, and cooking, turning raw carrots and herbs into tasty soups, I was both happy and melancholy as the hours became days which added up to years.

Henri's business thrived and he expanded his wares to include duck and pork pâté, some even with the epicurean treat of a truffle at the centre. He carved thick and thin slices of succulent pink ham and discovered a source of wild boar for even more sausages. He gained a reputation outside the village and on Saturdays we had visitors from other regions. He brought fame and prosperity to the village. His respect among our neighbours grew and he was chosen to be one of the *conseillers municipaux*, heading the names of those who were now responsible for our small community. He was elected by his colleagues to the post of Mayor and a flag was raised on the roof of Le Verger in honour of the man who lived there.

Meanwhile I filled our larder with jams, chutneys and preserves. I also put little luxuries on our neighbours' tables. Under his flag we led a quiet life but one profitable to our bodies. Lines might decorate our faces but good food comforted our bones with layers of flesh. We grew older.

-≪≪◆≫≫-

December heralded a particularly harsh winter. Henri developed a severe cold in the head. He remained indoors, ignoring his shop and his pies and sausages; leaving others to thank our Holy Mother for Her benefits. I prepared crusty bread and good chicken soup; travelled to the market town for soft cheeses and to the coast for fresh herrings. I fed him by the spoonful and encouraged his digestion with peppermint tea. At night, I warmed his bed with the old stone hot water bottle and his veins with hot milk and cognac. Once he was asleep, I enjoyed a tot.

Day by day the infection travelled through his body. His cheeks sank and the light in his eyes dimmed. Eventually, I went to the church, crossed myself, asked Our Lord to forgive me and prayed to his gentle mother for her help. If she heard, she either ignored me or her power was useless. Seven days later, my Henri's chest heaved, he uttered a loud groan as he spent his final breath and then he lay still. As I watched, his skin cooled and marbled yellow.

Outside the house, the daylight was dimming into evening; the sun sending a low beam of light through the window by the door. My view was of the church and the graveyard which was to be his new home. There was

Christmas Day to get through when I would open not just my presents but my husband's too.

That night I had no appetite and the guinea fowl stuffed with sweet apples stayed on the dish. Instead I fasted and kept vigil over Henri's body as the church bells tolled in the Christmas Eve Mass.

On the third day, December 27th, he left the house in his coffin.

His burial took place on a cold morning, with the promise of my sterile future frozen at the centre of it. The Requiem Mass offered me no solace. It was a beautiful service, the choir boys singing Fauré and, with a sincerity I had not known for years, I prayed for the grace to live my widow's years according to God's will.

The Virgin gave me her fixed smile but I ignored Her. I did not trust Her. She had betrayed me when I first needed Her and I had never been able to forgive.

-◄◄◄◆►►►-

The New Year is now with me and I have ordered work from the stone mason and the blacksmith.

The stone mason is a man with a head for business. 'I can offer you a two-for-one bargain on the headstone.'

I frowned. 'I am still alive.'

'Ah yes, of course. But we know your name and date of birth. Let me make a memorial wide enough for the two of you but carve the year of your death later. It will save you money and you can be sure that the space will come in useful one day.'

Amused by his morbid sense of value for money, I agreed. I would get a certain pleasure in visiting the grave and imagining my inevitable destiny carved in granite.

When I told the mason what I wanted he raised his eyebrows. 'Gold is impossible. No one puts solid gold anywhere. It will have to be gold leaf.'

'If that is the best you can do, I agree.'

'Can you pay for it?'

Whichever way I looked at the figures and did the sums I had plenty to keep my body and soul united for several more years. It would help to know how many years, but God likes His call to be a surprise. 'My husband's money will pay for it.'

He had a third obstacle to my plan. 'Aren't you afraid it will be stolen?'

'Not in this village. Everyone respected Henri. Anyway, you will see from my drawing that it will be tall and heavy. No one will be capable of lifting it from its base.'

Then he beamed at me. 'This is the most important commission of my life.'

In the meantime, my husband is in the ground while I pray he might be excused purgatory and speed his way to heaven.

-◄◄◄◆►►►-

Spring is here with its daffodils and primroses and Henri is resting under a grand marble slab surrounded by a delicate wrought iron fence. Above his head is a stone engraved with his name and dates and my name and my birth date. The space left for that final day in my life is a cold one and makes me shudder.

Easter is a time of re-birth and I change my heathen ways by attending mass each Sunday even if my devotion is out of fear that I might be eternally separated from my husband in death, him in heaven and me in hell. At least the devil's breath will be warm but, I have to admit, the company I will find there does not really appeal.

Every day I chat with my angel. Yes, my angel, for above Henri's tomb stands a winged statue, part man, part god, made by human hands but sublime nevertheless. At my particular request, he is four and a half cubits tall, the same height as the giant in the Bible, over two metres. This beautiful creature might be made of stone but he is gilded with the most precious metal known to man. When the sun shines, he glows. When the rain falls, his tears glisten. He is the reward Henri never gave me and he restores to me the pleasure my husband denied me. Whenever I walk past the tomb, although I can't resist a glance at that blank space, I am happy.

I still mourn the death of my son, the waste of such a young life, but I can now rejoice in the work my husband gave to the church and his village and the riches he left me. While I take the native flowers, cowslips followed by forget-me-nots chased by meadow daisies and honeysuckle to the minute grave of my child, to my husband's grave I present a bouquet from the florist, gaudy creations born of wealth and industry. I hope my angel shares my sense of humour.

The summer passes in a delightful way. I take my lunch of bread and cheese to the grave, open the gate in the fence and sit on the slab, eating the good food and taking a little wine, as the angel watches me. It's a good place and we are both happy to be there. Some days, I find I have too much and leave it for him to eat in the middle of the night when he's cold and hungry. In the morning, I wipe the marble slab clean of crumbs. As the days pass, I sit in the sun and tell my angel my secrets. I begin to love him.

-«««•»»»-

After gracing Henri's resting place with a vase of dahlias, a huge scarlet bloom veiling 'my' space, I take a little holiday at *Honfleur*, confident that my angel will watch over the tomb. I walk along the beaches and the harbour walls and feel the wind in my hair, the salt on my lips and my legs become as strong as iron. My skin is bronzed with sunshine and my hair bleached silver. I am alive and rejoice in my health. If I didn't know it was impossible, I would be fecund but, anyway, for that I need a man.

As the summer ends I am glad to return home to enjoy being in my kitchen, watching and smelling the onions and apples bubble into chutney; the figs into jam. Maybe, after the anniversary of Henri's death, I will invite the neighbours for punch and hot, sweet pies. I try a recipe or two and leave the results for my angel to feast on. By the time I visit him the next day the slab is clean. I realise that he is my son as Our Lord was the Virgin's son and not a day goes by when we don't sit with each other, quiet in our loving company. I love my angel more fully than I have ever loved a man and I feel complete.

I read Henri's name on the stone and mine, next to his, waiting for the inscription to be completed. I trace my name, Hélène Salomé, and imagine the date of my death. I torture myself with the knowledge that dying is yet another journey which I will not have in common with The Virgin. She was rewarded by not encountering death at all but merely discovering that her earthly life was ended as She was taken up to heaven by the angels. How long will it be before I must face the ordeal of quitting this world? This year? Next? Or the year after? I plead with my angel to enlighten me but he remains silent as he returns my love in a smile.

Autumn is late this year, the foliage clinging to the trees as I cling to my angel, their colours a pale imitation of his glorious sheen. When the leaves finally drop to languish in the mud, their shrivelled appearance cruelly reminds me of my infant Gabriel and his pale and sad demeanour the days before he left this world. Under the watchful gaze of my angel, I sweep the churchyard clean of the skeletal remnants of the ash, chestnut and black oak.

I restore my spirits by cooking since I have invited my neighbours to a celebration on Christmas Eve. I prepare hams painted with sugar crystals; fowls stuffed with local sausage and apple; quiches rich with cream and cheese; tarts savoury with pilchards and tomatoes or sweet with preserved plums. I bake a cake, nutritious with butter, eggs, raisins, dried apricots and almonds. I make a calming broth and a heady punch. I smooth tablecloths and napkins, polish glasses and clean plates. I am exhausted.

On the afternoon of my party I look out of the window and see that it is snowing. Great flakes are settling on the ground and on top of Henri's marble slab. I put wooden clogs over thick stockings and wrap my shawl around my head and shoulders and step outside.

The cold crisp air causes me to shiver and then cough. I am weary and slightly shivery and wish I had not been so ambitious with my preparations but preserved my strength.

The sight of my angel, with a cloak of pure white gossamer, cheers me and I sit as usual, refusing to contemplate the incomplete inscription as Christmas is a time of joy. The slab is as icy cold as water from the deepest well and I nibble on a portion of *mille-feuille* and drink from the glass of brandy which I brought for him. The hour of my party draws closer. But now I cannot bear the thought of it: the mass of people, their chatter and gaiety. Maybe even inebriation. My Henri would not have allowed it and I feel suddenly guilty and look up to my angel for sympathy.

He smiles at me and warms my heart while my flesh freezes. I sway a little in the cruel wind and it is as if I am drawing closer to him. Then he bends towards me, holding out his hand. I reach up and grasp him, our fingers touch. My living skin is numb whereas I sense his is warm and soft.

'Come with me,' he sings. His voice is sweeter than any choirboy's and I let my fingers wrap around his. He continues, 'Together we will leave this sad and cold place and fly directly to heaven to find warmth and everlasting joy.'

And love? Will we find love? Is that what my angel is promising me? Will he give me what I desire?

I glance at the empty space on the tombstone and wonder what my neighbours will carve there if I take this chance to journey to heaven without giving them the gratification of my dead body. The thought appeals to my sense of humour. I remain silent but nod to my angel.

He steps down from his plinth and gathers me in his arms. His lips on mine are as sweet as golden mirabelles.

My body is light as goose feathers and floats as the down fleeing the dandelion. I close my eyes and whisper, '*J'étais Hélène Salomé. J'ai quitté ce monde à...*'

Conflict

I stand straight-backed as if still on active service, as if being inspected by an officer.

Good posture keeps the body from trembling, protects against shock. And this morning I have had a shock. I have to speak to someone, anyone. I have a name here, printed on a small, white card. The details are only supposed to be used in an emergency but this is one.

The telephone number on the card is printed too damned small and I have to squint to read. 'Family liaison officer' and then a string of digits. He's far away this liaison officer, across county borders only nowadays they've done away with counties. As I push my finger into the numbers, I imagine his phone ringing, he's pressing the button, he's about to tell me if my lad is… His voice is distorted into robot speech. 'This is Captain Hardy. I can't take your call…'

Cursing the man, I press my thumb hard on the OFF. What's the point of having a family liaison officer if he doesn't pick up when he's needed? And I need him now.

The shaking in my legs returns and I sit heavily on the small, hard chair which my wife bought. It had a cushion but that seems to have been mislaid.

Meg used to sit on this chair and say, 'I'm waiting for our lad to come home. All this soldiering life is not for him.'

The doctor said she had a touch of dementia but I was having none of it. All she wanted was for our boy to be safe at home. And right now, I agree. I wish she was here with me now and then I am relieved she's not. I wouldn't put anyone else through this, certainly not the woman I loved.

I've left the television on in the living room and I can hear yet another announcement. Since the war in Iraq began, I've been turning the set on first thing. First ever war to be televised. Thought it was a gift, being able to follow the platoon, keep up with what they're doing. I think it's bloody marvellous how the TV people do it. Why don't the camera men get shot? Why are those ruddy red explosions always on the far side of the desert and not right at their feet?

That was until this morning. Now it's more like a curse. I usually sit and watch the fire and the flames with a calm detachment. Our men know what they're doing. They're the most professional fighters in the world. Not that we thought they'd have to face the enemy ever again. After all, we're all friends now. In Europe at least. No, a few months training in the jungle was all we expected, then we'd have them home on leave with stories to make us wonder.

But recently all that's changed. The world has grown smaller. We might have allies but the new enemy, so we're told, is in the Middle East.

There's more to my devotion to the TV than a silly old man watching war films for real. The screen offers me a lifeline to my grandson. Yes, he's out there, fighting for

Queen and Country and I'm the only one he's got to watch for him.

He lived with us, you see, our grandson. We looked after him. He was fifteen when his parents were killed in a road accident, when a bad winter turned into a dreadful one. He was old enough to choose and he chose us. We did our best by him, my wife and I. Insisted he went to college before going into the army. 'That way,' I said to him, 'You'll have something to rely on if you come out.'

But he didn't want to come out. He said to me, 'It's my life, Grandpa, I love it.'

We were both so proud of him. My wife spoke of him just before she died. 'Look after our grandson,' she whispered. 'But let him breathe. Let him be free.'

Now look where this freedom has got him.

-◄◄◄♦►►►-

The announcements have been coming on the hour since seven this morning. I'm beginning to dread the news which comes on the box in our living room. I loathe all machines. Small tanks they call them but they're really armoured cars. They go in first. Reconnaisance, they call it. I call it near suicide.

Fighting for patience, desperate to stay calm, I return to the lounge, to the striped wall-paper, the settee which needs recovering and my comfy armchair set directly in front of the tele. I go back to the pictures, to the voice-overs which betray no emotion. I used to tell myself no news was good news. Up to today it's been a true cliché. Now I don't know any more. At least they haven't got one of those smiley women with the red lips and flashy clothes. The announcer is wearing a sober suit and a navy-blue tie.

'There is still no further news of the friendly fire incident north of Baghdad. It is understood there are British casualties.'

Friendly fire. It is understood. What namby-pamby language. Why can't they just tell us straight how bad it is? *Casualties* could mean a twisted ankle or a burnt body. And which idiot exactly attacked his own side? Feeling impotent, I resort to every British man's answer to pain. I go into the kitchen, where my crumb-flecked plate still sits on the draining board, and I put the kettle on.

It's in the family, being in the army. My grandson was only six years old when I showed him his great-grandfather's medal: The Victoria Cross for valour. As he grew up, I'd let him take the medal out of the box as a reward for good marks in his school work. When he passed his GCSEs I said, 'You'll get a place in the army now. You'll be following in brave footsteps.' When the regiment accepted him, we played a little game, pinning the medal on his chest and pretending he'd won it for 'services beyond the call of duty.'

Never once did I imagine he'd be hurt. You don't, do you? If we thought our boys would be hurt we wouldn't let them go. As for being hit by their own side...

A further announcement has me scuttling back to the TV.

'We can now confirm that the unit north of Baghdad was hit by an American bomber plane. A British helicopter has picked up two injured men.'

I watch library pictures showing a helicopter flying across a city of squat buildings with flat roofs. In the distance fires burn the sand red. The sound track is the pop-popping of guns with an occasional explosion. I've watched this clip before, sure of it, but now this 'copter is carrying my grandson. Sure of it.

My tea is cold. I'm frightened and my upper lip is trembling.

The day he left, I drove him back to the barracks.

'I'll get out here, Grandpa,' he said once we were through the gates and had gone part way to his hut. Didn't want his mates to see him feather-bedded.

On the tarmac, we shook hands. I told him, 'Stiff upper lip, that's what it's all about. Don't flinch from duty. When it gets bad, you'll get through.'

'Be seeing you, Grandpa.' Then he turned and walked away.

But as I steered towards the exit, I could see him in the rear-view mirror, see that he'd turned and was watching me leave. How could I let him to go away to fight? Why wasn't I stopping him? Had the world gone mad? Just suppose he didn't come back. I couldn't just drive back into town, to my cosy house, not just like that. It was too easy and too impossible. I stopped the car, got out and ran back to him. Holding his shoulders with both hands, I kissed him on both cheeks. I had a lump the size of a football in my throat but I didn't cry. 'You'll make it lad,' I said. Then I left him.

And I believed myself. Until this morning. I know his unit. I know from the papers where they are. He's among those bombed and I want to know the damage. I want to know the worst.

I ring the liaison officer again. No change. I have time to make a fresh brew before the man in the dark suit is back on the screen. The tie is black.

'It has been confirmed that there has been one fatality as a result of the so-called friendly fire attack on a British unit north of Baghdad. The family has not yet been informed.'

The tea in my stomach churns with bile. It can't be him. He'll get through it. He will. He must. No one has rung me. He must be alive.

Then I remember. They don't ring if it's a death. They come round. A policeman and a specially trained ex-service man. It could be hours before I know.

The television is showing pictures of the type of plane thought to have done the damage: a bloody Yankee bomber. One of those fancy boys in blue has wiped out one of our tanks, put two men in hospital and killed my grandson. My boy's boy. The thought is out before I can stop it and I can feel my heart thumping and my blood flooding with adrenalin. My mouth is slack, my fingers cold and I can't be brave any more.

I know he's a busy man. I know there are other more important people than me. I know, if I wait long enough, I'll have my answer. But I can't wait. I have to know. I have to know about my own flesh and blood. The clear trill of the phone competes with the thumping in my chest. There's a pain in my heart and my throat is blocked with sobs but, when the ringing stops, when the officer says, 'Who is this?' I blurt out my name. 'Just tell me if it's my boy.'

The officer's voice, as he answers me, is steady, at first too efficient for compassion.

I listen to what he has to say in silence. I gulp and feel the bitter sweetness of undeserved relief.

But then the officer says, 'Be strong. Your grandson would want you to be strong.'

My tears come hot and much too wet. I manage a 'Thank you' before I hang up.

I sit on the small chair again and wish now I wasn't alone. I long for my wife to put her arms round me and love me. Because as I try to be glad I rang that special number for emergencies, I can't be. As I try to give thanks for my good news, I fail. As hard as I try to stem my tears they still pour out.

As I feel the sweep of thankfulness fill my heart, I know another man, with as much love for his family as I have ever had, is feeling the sick swirl brought by news too hard to bear, too terrible to comprehend.

For even as I am hearing my grandson is alive, I know another man is learning his boy is dead.

The Magic Answer

Hermione stood with her back to the horizon, grinning foolishly as the sea tickled her ankle bones. Her view was of the path running round the bay, stalls offering flip-flops and printed scarves, cafes providing sweet coffee and creamy pastries, before soft hills rose to become rocky crags and the deep, blue sky carried the eye up to the land of the gods.

She sighed. Pure magic.

And there he was, her very own Adonis, tall, dark and handsome waiting for her. The textbook perfect lover. If only...

It was some months ago when she'd taken a final look at the seductive scenery on her laptop screen. The photos were of a turquoise sea, a yellow, sandy cavern of rocks shielding the bay, even a mysterious ruined tower set amongst low, green shrubs.

And she'd clicked on 'Pay Now'.

When she told Theo he said, 'Greece! Great atmosphere for making a baby.'

She'd scowled.

-◄◄◄◆►►►-

With her business partner Clara, she ran a successful small enterprise from home. Her home as it happened. Together they made bespoke party dresses for girls from three to seven years old. Hermione made up the basic frocks, blue or red velvet for winter or pink patterned cotton lawn for the summer, while Clara decorated them as requested by the customer – silk trim to the puffed sleeves, braid around the hem or collar, matching or contrasting waist sashes. They were on to a winner. Once a customer ordered that cute little outfit for their three-year-old, she was a client for the next four years. A smash hit of an idea.

The last thing Hermione wanted was a baby keeping her awake all night or a toddler smearing sticky fingers on a roll of new material. No, she had her creative fulfilment with the dressmaking, her emotional reward with seeing the dresses on the children and the financial gain which would pay for a holiday at an exclusive resort.

When told of the plans, Clara had raised her eyebrows. 'Second honeymoon?'

'It won't quite be that,' Hermione said, remembering bed all morning and late night love with mouths tasting of Chinese take-away. But Greece. All those gods made drunk by wine and lust.

'You've plenty of time for babies,' was Clara's encouragement. 'Mind you, Mother Nature isn't on your side. Nymphs are the fertile ones, and maidens change into nymphs at puberty. Which for you must have been a while ago.'

'What've nymphs got to do with me?'

Clara coloured. 'I read classics and with your husband

being called Theo and you being Hermione, my mind ran on. Theo means God.'

'And Hermione?'

Her skin flushed. 'Was barren.'

Hermione felt a glimmer of hope. Was it an omen? A couple of days later, she'd made up her mind. She'd make a mad dash for the sun and the sea and let the sex persuade her god that lust was the ultimate goal for a happy marriage.

None of this she mentioned to Theo. After some quick revision on gods, maidens, nymphs and whatnots she understood that taking people by surprise was a key element in the mythical world. Icarus was taken by surprise when the sun melted his wings; she bet Narcissus had a hell of a shock when he turned into a flower and Achilles had no idea he'd be killed by an arrow in his heel. The somewhat morbid aspects of the stories, she decided, had nothing to do with reality.

-◄◄◄◆►►►-

On the first morning on the island, waking to the energy of the ocean and the cry of wild birds, she knew she'd done exactly the right thing. Also that she realised she was starving hungry. Rolls and honey were on her planned menu.

'Breakfast is rather a do-it-yourself activity.'

The voice, rather too loud and close to her ear, made Hermione jump in her skin. She was on a narrow path running along the back of the building, surveying the offerings set out on a small table: a wooden box for the teabags, mugs, a teapot, a jar of instant coffee and a packet of tea but no milk or rolls and certainly no honey. True they were staying in a hotel which offered rooms and breakfast but no other meals, but she'd expected more than this.

She turned round to find a woman with long loose hair, bleached into old straw by the sun, standing with her arms folded. Hermione reckoned her age to be about forty, thus a crone. 'Excuse me?'

The woman combed her hair from her face with her fingers. 'Welcome to the first meal of the day.'

Hermione adjusted the age to nearer fifty. 'This is supposed to be breakfast?'

'Our hostess is terribly laid back.' With one hand on her lower back as if it hurt her, she walked over to the table and opened the box. 'Here it all is. Mint, liquorice, rose, elderberry, nettle, help yourself.'

'No Darjeeling?'

The woman smiled. She had a tooth missing. Age upped to sixty. 'You're on a Greek island. Why should anything be ordinary?'

Settled at a round table on the terrace, the woman stirred five teaspoonfuls of sugar into her black tea. 'Getting a break from the kids?'

Which irritated Hermione beyond reason. 'Certainly not.'

'Ah', said the woman. 'You've come seeking fun and fulfilment.'

Hermione found herself telling the whole story, the love-at-first-sight, sex in a bedsit, her vision of never ending bed, booze and bingeing. 'Theo's a television cook. Apart from the sex we eat a lot.' She paused, feeling unfaithful, but so what? Theo was pushing her into something she didn't want. Not exactly loving, was it? 'I'm happy with the way things are. But Theo has this thing about babies.'

'He wants to create.'

'Cooking is creative.'

'But not permanent. He craves descendants.'

'Well I don't.'

'Let the magic of the island dispel his need of anything more than his lovely companion.'

Which sounded promising. 'Are you on holiday?' Although, as she said it, Hermione knew that walnut tan on the woman's skin meant more than a quick break.

The crone shrugged. 'Forgotten when I arrived. Can't leave now. I'm embedded.' The woman laughed a cackle and her face cracked into a million lines.

The phrase *three score years and ten* jumped onto Hermione's head. 'I'm Hermione.'

The woman leaned forward and took her hand. 'Daphne. The nymph who wouldn't submit to a man.'

Theo's feet flipped-flopped onto the terrace, carrying a mug, dripping coffee onto the stones. 'Is this it? Make your own coffee and not even the proper stuff?'

Hermione pulled back her hand. 'It's a Greek thing. Being laid back.'

'I'm getting in a few drinks. Come back to bed later?'

They watched his back as he stomped off.

Daphne winked at Hermione. 'I see the problem. Does he party?'

Hermione shrugged. 'Suppose. Why?'

'You ask a lot of questions. Disbelief can get in the way.'

Daphne finished her coffee. 'There's a party each Saturday. As it happens, this week's party is rather special.'

Hermione stopped herself asking why. Not that she was taking any notice of the old crone but she was here now and you never knew.

Daphne was staring at the sea as if monsters were about to appear, ones with seven heads. 'It's the autumn equinox. The moon will slip into the sea and women will reign supreme.' She held Hermione's hand again. 'Not long and we'll have no need of men or gods. We women will be on our own.' She gave Hermione's hand a hard squeeze before pushing it back.

Mad as a hatter. Hermione stood up. 'I'd better find Theo and share a retsina with him. Or several. One glass makes him feel sexy. Four and he's in bed but fast asleep.'

'Before the sun goes down, we'll take a little walk.' The crone nodded towards the hills.

'OK if I bring Theo?'

A deep frown scarred Daphne's face. 'I was hoping for a girls' talk but never mind. We've got plenty of time.'

-◄◄◄◆►►►-

By six o'clock Hermione was gently relaxed. They'd spent the day eating bread, cheese and grapes, drinking retsina. They'd also held hands while jumping the waves and snuggled on the sand. Hermione lay face down while Theo smoothed cream over her shoulders and her back, undoing her bikini strap and only stopping when his fingers were stretching the elastic of her bottoms. He then rushed her up to their room for an energetic consummation of their holiday selves, afterwards suggesting a stroll along the seafront to investigate tavernas and cocktail bars for a sun-downer. With no mention of babies.

Hermione had never been so happy. Food didn't matter anymore. She'd live on drink and love. A true Greek nymph.

They'd stopped in front of a bar, open to the sea and with rush seats outside on the pavement when the clatter of wooden sandals and a 'Coo-ee!' made them look along the path.

Theo put his hand above his eyes. 'It's that old bag you were with earlier. Can't imagine what you found to talk about.'

Hermione put her sunglasses on to hide her betrayal. 'Ah.'

'Ah what?'

'I'm supposed to be going for a walk with her.'

'What the hell for?'

Hermione shrugged. 'She was friendly to me when you were still in bed this morning. You don't have to come.'

'And let you go off with that scruffy old tramp? I might not be a knight in shining armour but I hope I'd look after you better than that.' He grinned at her. 'Anywhere you go, I go.' He crooked his arm for her to take.

Hermione giggled. 'Like an old married couple.'

'Lovely evening.' Daphne, wearing a long turquoise skirt and a sleeveless silver top, too scanty for her thin body, was holding a wrap of patterned fabric, blue shells against gold, and a large bag, with a pair of secateurs sticking out. 'A stroll to the top of the cliff? There's a rather special place I want to show you. Absolute peace.'

Theo whispered, 'Don't encourage her.'

'She can't do us any harm. Her name's Daphne.'

'The man hater. Doesn't want me around then. Pity. I'm staying.'

-◄◄◄◆►►►-

The steep climb took them past a taverna already open for dinner, the open spit enticing them with chicken, garlic and rosemary. Hermione could feel Theo willing her to call a halt to this crazy expedition but she walked determinedly after Daphne, up and up, until they reached a place where wild flowers with thick stalks and soft yellow buds grew among the rocks.

Daphne took a deep breath and threw her arms open, releasing scents of lavender and thyme soured by old skin and talcum powder. She pronounced, 'A shrine. This is a holy place. Look.' She pointed to a church with a bell tower, perched on a slab of rock. 'The villagers ring that bell when someone dies.'

Theo grimaced. 'Gruesome. I'm going back.' And without waiting for a response from Hermione, he went, taking long strides down to the village.

Daphne put an arm round Hermione's shoulders. 'Let him go. You must understand this place.' And she threw her arms wide, embracing the blue sky, the tawny rocks and the yellow flowers. 'Follow me.'

She walked towards the edge of the rock and stopped.

Hermione followed until she could see, below her, a deep chasm, the landscape surrounded by rock. A roofless cavern. Far away, the ground was black as if it had been burnt. In the middle of the space stood a narrow block of granite. An altar. She saw a goat, its throat cut clean, blood flooding the stone. And then it was gone. A vision.

Daphne was standing close to her, much too close.

Hermione inhaled the stink of urine and stale lipstick.

Her new friend's voice was low and breathy. 'That's where the answer to the mystery lies. And dilemmas are solved. Down there.'

Down there was another world, one of nymphs and gods. And sacrifices. The steep drop made Hermione dizzy. Surely they weren't going down now? The climb looked treacherous. Daphne wouldn't do her any harm, would she? Hermione glanced at her. Definitely an old crone. She shuddered. 'What mystery?'

'How to manage without the men.' Daphne cackled at her own cleverness. 'You'll see. There's to be a gathering. Saturday night. Sweet music, exotic food, wine of the gods.'

'I thought that was water. I'll never get Theo to party on water.'

'Mead. Leave everything to me. Just be down there on Saturday as the sun sets.' She gave Hermione a little push, so that her toe was at the very edge and she could sense the drop, the possibility of taking Theo down to that cavern, to the darkness and the moonlight, to the excesses of island life.

Hermione realised, in spite of the apparent madness, her anticipation was all the more exciting for pleasure being mixed with suspense.

-◄◄◄◆►►►-

The next day she spent hours swimming in the balmy water, across the bay and back. Theo rose late as usual and came to the water's edge to watch her. His admiration rewarded her with a long session of cuddling, stroking, kissing and lots more, letting go completely, reckoning other hotel guests were all out sunbathing.

With Theo, she walked the path along the shore line, riffling through rails of shifts of silk and scarves of gauze. Slippery to touch. Tantalizing to see. Theo bought her a sheer triangle cut from a rainbow to protect her skin from the sun. Lunches, eaten at tables under umbrellas made from woven leaves, were crunchy bread, juicy fruit and bitter, dark coffee. Later, in the afternoon, smaller cafes offered snacks of spicy cake with green tea. Dinner was often a bar-b-que of the sweet meat of lamb ribs, with scented rice and green oil on crisp salad leaves. More coffee kept them awake for the midnight tryst with Eros.

-◄◄◄◆▸▸▸-

Friday was a day of foreboding. Clouds hung over the bay and huge, wide-winged birds circled above their heads. They both drank too much at lunch time and returned to bed. But Hermione couldn't sleep. A heavy worry sat on her, a fear of what the next day would bring. With Theo deep asleep, she rolled out of bed. Slowly. Softly. Silently. Until she was safely outside. The sky was still clouded. Quickly she trotted along the path, past stalls and late holidaymakers, then turned and ran up the grassy slope towards the rocky ledges, to end up above the cavern.

She peered down. Behind the altar, preparations for a bonfire were taking place.

Youths dragging gnarled logs, branches of dry leaves, stacking dark peat. A man with seven goats, with brown and cream markings and neat, black hooves, puts a pan-pipe between his lips. Dancing begins. A jig. Feet lifting. Toes pointing. Knees bending. The goats stop nibbling and watch. Bemused. As if being entertained. And then the man stops whistling to look up. And bows. To her? Her fear returns. Thunder claps. Run. Round sharp edges. Slips on steep path. Light dipping towards the sea. Must get back. No torch. Mustn't fall. Path softer now. Flowers replace thistles. Rooftops become closer.

She was back on the tarmac path. A sigh of relief. Already there were lights above doors and the evening waves made huge, angry splashing noises as they broke on the shore.

She stopped for just a minute and breathed deeply. She was still safe.

Suddenly in front of her was the goat man. Grinning. Winking. At her. Younger than she'd thought. He bowed again as if he knew more than she did. Then, with his goats following, he skipped and twisted away, round a corner. Her heart beat hard, her chest was sore.

At supper, Theo was grumpy towards her. 'You could have been hurt. Lost in the dark. Wouldn't have had a clue where to start looking.'

'I wasn't alone. The goat man was there.' Big mistake.

'You mean that dirty old man tootling at his mangy herd.'

'Not old. Not dirty. And the goats are rather sweet.'

'Retsina?'

Later, much too drunk, sleep. Dreams of hot bodies. One of them furry. Silent orgasm.

-‹‹‹◆›››-

Saturday rose dusky to warm into the gloaming. The sun was eclipsed by a huge red cloud. Blood in the sky. The heat was suffocating enthusiasm out of them. They spent the day quietly, trying to read but their eyes wanted to slumber until the sun cooled and slipped into the sea.

They decided on a snooze before the fun began. As he drifted off, Theo said, 'They've asked me to go early. Some man thing about the bonfire.' He tapped the side of his nose as if it were a big secret.

She wanted to know who exactly had asked him but he'd already transformed into Hypnos, the lord of sleep.

-‹‹‹◆›››-

When she woke, it was already dusk. Theo was not with her. Hermione dressed in a long, silk shift of colours mixing the sea with the sky; sand with spilt blood.

Daphne was waiting on the path, her body swathed in black chiffon. Mournful.

'Theo's disappeared.' Nevertheless, Hermione was excited. Agitated? No. Stimulated.

Daphne handed her a glass of something green. 'A potion. It won't hurt. Just opens your eyes to possibilities.'

Hermione expected it to be bitter but she was wrong. Sweet was too light a word. Heavenly wasn't.

'Take my hand.' And the crone held out her long-nailed fingers.

They stumbled upwards. Hermione suspected her vision was blurred but no, below she saw clearly the fire.

She allowed Daphne to lead her down into the chasm. Towards the chaos. For it was chaos. The bonfire was huge and rose above her like a burning tower. Closer and she felt the heat and heard crazy music, the notes up and down and round and round. The dungeon of Hades. And there was the Pan Man. No longer a mortal. Sinewy arms, nimble fingers, hairy ribbed skin above dark belly button. Finally, fur thighs, straight calves, no spare flesh, neat hooves, clip-clopping on the rock.

The notes whistled in the air, around her head. The devil's tune.

Daphne took her hand. They danced lightly, as if spirits. Hermione couldn't feel her feet or the ground under her. Only the warm air, cushioning her, almost lifting her, up and down, up and down.

'I should dance with Theo.'

'The King must die.' Scrawny arm lifts. Finger points.

The flames twirl. Twigs crack. Fiery fragments blow. Drift down to Hermione. Land on her hair. Burning. She senses roasting and shifts her gaze to the top of the bonfire. And there he is. Her beloved the sacrifice. Hair lit orange. Rays of the sun. His face glows; limbs jerk and jiggle. A crazy tango. His eyes? Are not there. He is gone.

Above them, the church bell tolls.

Daphne's hand tugs. 'We don't need men.'

'But the baby…' Did she say that? Now there could

not possibly be a baby. Tears ran down her face. She was a monster.

Daphne smiles, baring chipped teeth. 'It will arrive. We are all it will need. We will care for it. Together.'

The heat. The smell of roasting meat. It is too much. Hermione is confused. Scared. She doesn't understand. Her head is too light. She needs help. Pulling free of Daphne, she turns away.

To the goat man. Who guides her away from the fire, up the cliff face, across the grass, under thick, smoked sky. Then down the path to the village. They turn a corner. Hermione lets him rule her. She wants to be with him. A stable. Inside warm, musky. Low munching. Hay. His touch, his hands revealing her body. Softly, with not a scratch on her naked skin, she surrenders. Hermione is re-born, crowned a mother.

-‹‹‹•›››-

They buried Theo's bones in a shallow grave on top of the mountain. Then piled yellow stones. Daphne prevented Hermione from attending. 'You don't want a changeling.'

She didn't. Or a kid with fur on its legs.

Daphne guarded Hermione night and day, feeding her milk and honey, vowing to be godmother.

While the goat man waited. Grinning.

Old Skin and Cabbage

The room smells of old skin and cabbage.

I have no idea whose lounge this is. Certainly not mine. Much too big and the chairs are the kind they have on TV adverts with old people pressing buttons to make the footrests go up and down. I'm reminded of that bit in the Bible about putting away childish things. I shudder. Saint Paul is another man I'm not keen on.

I am sitting in my usual place by the window. In the garden, the sun has abandoned the afternoon and the wind is blowing the leaves from the trees. It must be cold out there but I am safe this side of the glass. Now, this young woman has arrived. She's wearing spectacles and carrying a cloth bag with two bamboo rings for handles.

'Hello, my name is Amy,' says the young woman.

'That's an old fashioned name,' I reply.

'They come around.' She laughs as if she's made a joke. 'I'm a student. Are you happy if I chat to you? Ask you a few questions?'

Happy indeed. As if I were some dumb animal to be bought over with a saucer of milk or a fresh bone.

She perches on an upright chair as if her bottom is stuck to the edge of the seat and rummages around in her bag. She produces a biro and a form printed in headed columns. The form has my name on it.

My visitor smiles. 'Your daughter said you wouldn't mind helping me.' Her mouth is full of teeth which is more than mine is. Without explaining she demands, 'Tell me about the time you went to the zoo.'

I wish she would go away, I didn't come here to be pestered. I don't want to be rude so I say, 'I have no idea what you are talking about.'

She pushes her spectacles up her nose and stares at me, owl like. 'Shall I jog your memory?'

I don't mind playing her game.

'You were in a large auditorium.' Amy stops. Her biro hovers over her pad. 'What does auditorium mean?'

I'm not a fool. 'It's a large room with seats in it. Used for talks, lectures, that kind of thing.'

She puts a tick in a column marked *Vocabulary*.

'I can read upside down,' I announce. Amy's blush makes her quite pretty, not at all bird like. I say, 'I could tell you about an owl.'

She leans forward, a teacher pleased with a student. 'Your daughter said you were at a presentation with your husband.'

I'll be having a word with Sarah when next I see her. 'My husband is called Richard. He's not here right now.'

She scrunches up her lips as if I have said a dirty word and puts a tick in the column headed *Confused*.

That makes me angry on Richard's account. People often think he's confused. 'Richard's deaf, you know.'

She nods. 'He was thinking of buying a new hearing aid and the company making them had an owl as their logo.'

'I'm not sure what a logo is.' My ignorance earns me a tick under *Self Confidence*.

Amy keeps talking. 'The event was held at the zoo, in a large tent. An owl flew around before the heavy sell started.'

I don't understand 'heavy sell' but let her chat away.

'The owl flew across your heads until the keeper attracted it back to its perch with a live mouse for its supper.'

I don't like the sound of that. 'You've made a mistake. I'd remember watching an owl eat a mouse.' I give her a look. Sometimes I give the blue-frocks a look when they take away my dinner plate before I've finished my meal. 'How do you know all of this?'

'Your daughter told me. She said you both enjoyed the occasion.'

'Sarah should know better than to gossip to strangers.' The sharp tone of my voice cuts through any harmony we've established.

One of the blue-frock brigade wheels in the tea trolley.

'That cake looks good,' says Amy, too brightly, as if cake were a special treat.

I come to the conclusion she's a bit dippy but she nips up and fetches me a cup of tea. It has sugar in it and the warm, sweet liquid in my mouth brings a taste from childhood, an unexpected pleasure. Suddenly I want to tell Amy a story.

'When I was about six, my father took me to the zoo. I was wearing a pink gingham dress.' I pause. 'Gingham means checked. My father bought me a lemonade, I rode on a camel and we watched the chimpanzees' tea party. A female wearing an apron poured tea from a pot just like a real mother. All the children were watching and laughing at

81

the chimps' antics.' I laugh and my cup rattles on its saucer.
A blue-frock takes it away.

'They don't have those tea parties any more,' Amy tells
me. 'They don't like people laughing at animals.'

'But they like people watching owls eat live mice?'

She gives me a sudden, sharp look, as if I've got
something wrong again.

I must clear things up. 'When Richard and I came out
of the tent, it was dark. The zoo was empty apart from the
animals. The night was clear, the stars bright. It wasn't cold
and the air smelt musty, thick with the heat of animals' bodies.'

Amy's scribbling like mad. I have to make her see exactly
what it was like, to make her understand what it is to be
alone and shut up at night. 'I watched a leopard in his cage.
He was wide awake and prowling up and down. There was
a sheet of glass between us and he came right up to it and
we stared at each other through the glass as if we might be
friends. I felt sad for him with no family in there. Owls were
flying and hooting; bats were flitting and flapping inside
their cages. It seemed to me they were all trying to escape, to
get back to the life they had when they were free. I was upset
and asked Richard to take me home.'

'You remember all that?' Amy frowned. 'Earlier you said
you were at the zoo with your father.'

'Not that visit.' She does try my patience, this Amy person.
'That was years ago. I'm talking about the time I went with
Richard. Richard's deaf you know. What are you writing?'

Her eyes flicker as if she's unsure. 'I've written that
although you have some short term memory loss your long
term memory is excellent and you seem well.'

'I'm perfectly well. And I haven't forgotten anything.'

My new friend puts down her biro with a snap, stows her pad of forms in her floppy bag and gives a great sigh as if everything I've said is wrong. 'I'll see you again in a week's time.'

'I won't be here next week. Richard will come to take me home.'

The woman's face flickers is if she is in pain. She holds one of my hands. 'You live here now.'

I snatch my hand away. 'I don't live here. I'm at some sort of house party. Richard will come for me. He needs me.'

Amy leaves me to eat my cake.

I enjoy afternoon tea. Sometimes I help the blue-frocks. One of the women ties a pinny on me. The pinny is pink checked just like the frock I wore when I was a little girl and I feel at home.

--‹‹‹•›››--

If that Amy person comes this morning, she won't find me lazing in a chair. I hope she does since I'm dressed for a visitor, in my pleated skirt and this smart, red cardigan. And certainly not carpet slippers with their fluffy collars. Here comes that head woman and she *has* got Amy with her. Wearing black as if she's at a funeral. Mind you, half the people here should be dead.

'Hello again, Mrs Webster.' Amy sits down alongside the table. 'Doing a jigsaw puzzle.'

'I am.'

'Shall we go on with our investigations?'

I drop a piece of puzzle and bend down to pick it up. I need time to think. Her words sound too official. When I am sitting straight I ask, 'Are you from the police?'

'Good gracious me no,' she says. 'Nothing for you to worry about.'

She laughs. Odd, the things people find funny. Nothing funny about the police. 'It would help if you told me what exactly we are working on.' I watch her scrabbling in her pocket. 'One of the women in blue will have a pen.'

Amy found her pen and put a tick in the column headed *Awareness*.

I am determined to find out what this is all about. I need to sleep at night. 'Why exactly are you doing all that ticking?'

'You're helping me with data on the elderly.'

'Don't you need my permission?'

Amy puts a tick under the column *Rights of the Citizen*. 'Your daughter said you wouldn't mind talking to me.'

'I'll be having a word with Sarah when she next comes in.'

'You know where you are?'

'I'm at a house party until Richard collects me.'

A woman wearing a blue overall puts two mugs of coffee on a small table. Amy shakes her head at the offer of a shortbread biscuit while I take mine and bite into it.

A tick under *Appetite* before Amy prompts, 'So, you were at the zoo recently?'

'I was with Richard.'

'Now *I'm* confused. Your daughter told me *she* had taken you to the zoo. Your daughter told me you saw an owl there.'

'Max.' I'm triumphant. 'His name was Max.'

'You remember his, I mean, its name?'

I think 'evidently' and say, 'I saw the owl with Richard first. Richard's deaf you know.' I glance around the room and then shudder. 'If you are from the police you could arrest the old man in that chair. He's wet his trousers. I had a dog once and when he started wetting the carpet I had him put down.'

But she didn't even turn round to look. 'You seem to remember your husband's deafness very well.'

'You should be interviewing him. People take him for confused. He'd make an interesting subject.'

Amy reaches out and takes my hand in exactly the same way as she did before. 'Richard is dead.'

I snatch back my hand. 'You're wrong. Quite wrong.'

She closes her file. 'Don't get upset. I don't blame you for...'

'Blame?' I stand up. I don't like this. I don't want to lose my temper so I'll just calm down by closing and unclosing my fists. I don't really want to hit Amy. 'There's nothing to blame me for.' I don't care that I am shouting now. Everyone in the room is looking at me, as if expecting a drama. 'Richard could be quite irritating at times. He was deaf you know.'

A blue frock is coming across the room. Amy turns to her. 'I seem to have upset Mrs Webster.'

The blue frock puts a hand on my arm. 'Now Mrs Webster. We don't want any trouble, do we?'

I shake her off. 'It's not me who makes trouble. Richard's deafness was nothing but trouble. Anyway, he's dead now.' And I sit down.

The blue frock asks Amy if she wants to 'give it a miss for today' but she says she wants to 'make some progress'.

I get back to my puzzle.

Amy sits back down and leans over the table. 'It's ages since I did one of these.'

'I don't want help.' I find the piece I am looking for and put it in with a pat. 'I can't stand it when someone else puts the best bits in. Richard does that.'

Amy seems occupied with her form.

Suddenly, I need to say, 'I want to put things right.'

'How?'

'Last time, I wasn't very helpful, was I? I told you about my visit to the zoo when I was a little girl and about the time I went there in the evening with Richard but I pretended I couldn't remember the day my daughter took me.' I pick up a piece of puzzle. 'Now I know where this goes. I've just spotted the gap. But it's moved.'

Amy drinks her coffee. 'Why did you pretend?'

'I was cross with Sarah for getting me into these investigations.'

'Do you remember better today?'

I give her a sharp look. 'I just said. I was pretending.'

'Do you pretend very often?'

'When it suits me.' I lean closer to her and whisper. 'I don't want everyone to hear my business. Especially about Richard.' I add another piece of puzzle. 'We were at the zoo because he needed hearing aids. It could be irritating his deafness. I had to say everything at least twice and even then he didn't always take notice. Sometimes I could have hit him.'

'I thought you were telling me about the visit with your daughter?'

'I need that last piece of the thatched roof.'

'The zoo?' Amy prompts.

'The company promoting the aids used an owl as a logo. I knew they were expensive, but I had no idea how much until the salesman told us.' I search for the next piece, find a section of a green gate and put it in. 'I like puzzles. It's comforting when things fit together.'

'How long have you been living in this home?'

'Since Richard died. Why?'

'Usually people come here because they can't look after themselves.'

'I can see that.'

'But not you?'

'I have my reasons for being here. Do you want to know about the hearing aids or not?'

'Are they important?'

'I'd say so. Two thousand pounds important. How expensive is that?'

'You didn't want Richard to buy them?'

I shrug. 'He said he needed them. Drove me mad. I could have killed him.' I can't help it, I bring my fist down on the table, making the pieces of the jigsaw jump.

Amy spots the missing piece of thatch and puts it in.

I stare at the puzzle. 'What's this?'

'It's your jigsaw.'

'Not anymore.' I push the half completed picture off the table, sending the pieces all over the carpet.

A blue frock comes over. 'I thought she was having a good day.'

Amy crouches to help the woman. While they are scrabbling for pieces, they whisper. As well as reading upside down, I have sharp ears. Amy is asking the blue frock if I have dementia.

'Don't ask me. They're all difficult from time to time. Mrs W is no worse than any of them.'

'Did you ever meet her husband?'

'Oh no. By the time she came here, he'd passed away.' The two women stand up. 'You'd like another coffee, wouldn't you dear?'

'Don't call me dear. I'm Mrs Webster to you.'

Amy sat down again. 'Would you like to talk about Richard?'

I grip her on the arm. I have to make her understand. 'Not so loudly. I don't want everyone hearing. I'm going to tell you something very important.'

Amy fumbles with her form but doesn't tick any columns.

'I went to the zoo three times. Once when I was a little girl. Once with Richard and once with my daughter. It smells in the zoo. Like this place. Only the zoo smells of hay and this place smells of cabbages.'

Amy is still listening.

'By the time I went with my daughter, Richard was dead.'

'Did you enjoy your outing?'

As if all I have to do is to enjoy things and that makes it all right. I slam down my mug, spilling brown liquid. 'I don't know what Sarah was thinking of.'

'Bringing back happy memories of your husband?'

'Richard? I didn't have many happy times with him. Richard was deaf, you know.'

'You told me.'

I pitch my voice a couple of decibels higher. 'People have no idea. Living with a deaf man can drive you insane. Two thousand pounds indeed. That pays for this place for two months.' Then I drop to a whisper. 'I'd visited this place. I had it all worked out.'

Amy smiles as if she understands me. 'What did you have all worked out?'

'That I didn't want to live on my own.'

'You visited after Richard had died?'

'You are slow. Two thousand pounds. I was thinking of my move here before he was dead. I like to be organised.'

'How could you? He was only deaf.'

'Only deaf! Have you any idea, of course no one has, no one can understand how difficult it can be, no idea at all, just think, living with a man you can't have a conversation with, who never answers you or never hears the simplest thing or can't watch TV or listen to the radio, just think...'

'Richard is dead now.'

I feel strangely calm. My turn to smile. 'I said I had something important to tell you but you must promise to keep it to yourself. No one else has guessed.'

'Guessed what?'

'I'm pretending.' Ah, ha. Now she's stumped. 'That's the way to do it. To pretend. I fooled Sarah and I'm fooling you.'

'About what?'

'They mustn't find out.'

'What?'

'Richard was deaf you know.'

Amy takes a deep breath. 'Mrs Webster, you have me beat. I have no idea what to report back...'

'Just as long as you don't tell them about Richard.'

'That he was deaf?'

Heavens, she's dim. Who employs these people? They should be shot at birth. 'Don't be daft. Who'd want to know that?' I reach up, take her hand and pull her closer to me. For just a second Amy looks as if she is about to be sick but I'm sure I don't smell. My skin is old, I'll give her that. If anything smells, it's the cabbage. She can listen to me for once.

'Richard fell down stairs. Head over heels, all the way from the top to the bottom. Broke his neck, as anyone would know he would.' My voice sounds like an old crone's.

'Two thousand pounds, indeed. Richard was deaf, you know…'

The Dance

The dance was to be the next day. So why is she so happy today?

For surely all the excitement will be in the event, the music, the pretty dresses, the buffet and their partners? Celebrating mid-summer is always special but to be just seventeen and attending a dance...

It's exciting just to stand on the bridge with her two best friends, to wonder, to imagine, to plan what might happen, to exchange ideas as the three of them gaze into the river, flowing deep, as deep as their dreams.

Astrid is the only one of the young women not covering her hair and it flows down her back, its strawberry blonde tint a warm contrast to the chilly, green water. Surely now is when it begins, this early evening tryst with her friends, as she stands apart from the other two, separate in her thoughts.

'I shall need a short beau,' Gudrun's saying. 'No other woman will want him so I can have him and we will match our steps and dance all evening.' She pauses. 'Except for the buffet. We shall enjoy tasting the salmon and the apple cake.'

'You should eat less cake,' Johanna says, poking her friend in the waist. 'You're getting fat. No man wants a tubby wife. You'll get round enough when you are with child.'

'Thank you,' retorts Gudrun. 'I'm not that keen to marry the first partner I find. We do not often have the chance to enjoy dancing and I will give myself up to the lure of the violins, to their sweet strings as the fiddlers weave their fantasies.'

'Don't enjoy your pleasures too openly,' warns Johanna, 'or the good women will say you are not respectable.' And she frowns as if she'll share the burden of guilt. 'What about you, Astrid? Will you be looking for a husband? Will you wed as young as your mother did?'

For it was well known in the village that Astrid's mother was only just fifteen when she accepted a proposal. He was the headmaster of the school, with his own house already and the good people of the church approved of the young woman who settled down quickly, became an obedient wife and gave no reason for tittle-tattle.

Astrid throws back her head and calls to the clouds, 'I am searching for love. When I find it I will take it whatever it brings.'

'Hush,' says Johanna. 'All the people will hear and think you shameless. Is that what you want?'

'I want an explosion in my heart. I want to drown in my love as if I were drowning in this river, speeding away on the current to a life of passion.'

Johanna *Phfff'd*. 'Rubbish. You want to be more careful. I've heard there's a stranger staying at the inn, a visitor from far away. No one knows who he is or where he comes from but he has dark skin and wild eyes.'

'Now who's being romantic?' scoffs Gudrun. 'Wild eyes, indeed. I suppose he will arrive at the dance in a black coach and horses, snatch up the first girl he sees and lock her in his castle.'

'At least that's an adventure.' Astrid sighs. 'But don't let's quarrel. Let's walk and talk of our dreams while we have them, for I am so unaccountably happy. I must share my joy with you and tomorrow we will go to the dance with one ambition.'

'Which is?' Johanna demands.

'To enjoy the music and to fulfil our fantasies.'

In her room, before she goes to bed, Astrid takes the dress she's to wear the following evening down from its hanger and holds it before her. Her reflection in the mirror pleases her. She's the tallest of the three, slender with a small waist. The gown of white silk is cut on the cross to emphasise her taught body, but the sleeves to the wrists are modest as is the high neck. A cream coloured layer of chiffon floats over the silk. It's patterned with gold marks as if a painter has loaded his brush with fairy dust and flicked it on the fabric. Finally, there's the belt. Golden leather with a round buckle. It will clench her waist tighter than any lover could.

With one hand she clutches the dress and, with the other, she gathers her hair in a bunch and pushes it up behind her head. There. Her face suddenly looks beautiful, her high cheekbones catching the light. She bites her lips bringing the blood to the skin and rolls them together. She feels a woman and the next night she will act a woman.

There's a tap on her door. 'I hope you are in bed, Astrid,' calls her mother. 'It might still be light but it's late. You need your sleep.'

'Yes, Mama.'

Later, she lies with her head on the pillow, the curtains pulled back, and watches the sky, the still warm glow of the midnight sun, the magical mid-summer light. She knows her happiness comes from a strange magic and that, at the dance, she will surrender to the enchantment.

-᪥᪥᪥᪥᪥-

Next day the hours sit heavily. Astrid's mother, preparing food for the buffet, is not short on commands to her daughter. 'Peel those apples and, when you have finished, fillet those herrings, cut them into small pieces and put them in the marinade. When you have done that…'

'I shall wash my hair and rinse it in vinegar to make it shine.' And Astrid sees her mother smile. 'You still feel it, mother. You remember the excitement you felt on the night you met father.' Astrid catches her round the waist and waltzes her round on the kitchen tiles.

The older woman pushes youth away from her. 'Just do your work and remember no man favours a brazen hussy and if he does he is no good. You are my eldest child and I long to see you happy.'

'So we agree.' Astrid kisses her on the nose and picks up the paring knife, all the time wondering about this stranger who is in their midst.

She's obedient enough to rest in the afternoon but her

dreams are disturbed by a dark presence, a shadow which both beguiles and repels her. Neither man nor beast, almost a spirit but for the voice which whispers in her ear, 'I want you Astrid. Come with me.'

Still, she wakes refreshed, slips her dress over her head and snaps fast the clasp of the belt. Then she secures her hair in a knot at the back of her head. 'There,' she says out loud, 'I will be the belle of the ball tonight and I will dance until I have no breath left in my body.'

But just as she's leaving, her mother calls to her. 'Wait. I've heard about this man from foreign parts staying at the hostelry. Somehow, he has a ticket for the dance although no one will admit to selling him one.'

Astrid shrugs. 'Well?'

'That is it,' replies her mother. 'It's not so good and several mothers are worried for their daughter's reputation so they are to be chaperoned by their fathers.'

'Oh please mother do not think like them. I will be with Johanna and Gudrun who are both wise and sensible. Are they not guardians enough?'

'It is more important to say that I trust in your prudence, Astrid. Especially,' she adds, 'as your father is too old to be sitting around in draughty halls until late at night.' And she kisses her daughter farewell.

-«‹‹•››»-

The dance is held in the largest room of the Radhus and, while the musicians tune their Hardanger Fiddles, Astrid, Johanna and Gudrun watch the other village girls arrive, preening themselves. And then the young men, more shyly, keeping together, muttering and pretending they're only in the room by accident and are not wanting to dance at all. But as the lead violinist strikes up a chord, one of the youths breaks away and claims Astrid for the first dance.

Her heart jumps. But she's to be disappointed for the youth is a plodder and takes her round the room in a desultory way, now and then stepping on her toes. She holds her head high and smiles, pretending to be enjoying herself but all the time looking at the door, watching for the arrival of the dark-skinned man.

The waltzes and the polkas follow rapidly and Astrid is spun round until her head whirls. She spots Gudrun dancing solidly with one man, a little older than the others, and she guesses her friend will be claimed in marriage before the night is finished. Johanna does not dance so much but helps serve the buffet, pleasing the women and gaining the admiration of the men looking for a reliable wife.

Astrid wishes her friends well but she takes another glass of wine and then another as she waits.

At last he arrives. A tall man wrapped in a cloak which he lets drop onto a chair. With boots that click on the wooden floor he makes straight for the bar to ask for whisky. He sits, watching the youngsters. But his interest seems focused on the women, both young and older. His stare is cool, appraising, as if he desires a special partner, an otherness.

Astrid shivers.

Hastily, as if to mask a phantom invading the room, the musicians take up their instruments and play a jig. Astrid taps her feet in time to the beat and waits. She knows he will come.

He bows low, holding out his hand. 'Will you do me the honour?'

She says nothing but steps into his arms, charmed.

Jigs are followed by waltzes followed by polkas. His arms hold her gently at first but then tighter as the music increases the pounding of their hearts. They never make a false step. There is no stepping on toes, no wrong moves and Astrid lets her body be taken over by his, her flesh bond with his. It's as if her bones have melted.

She loses track of the time, of the other dancers, eventually even of the music. It doesn't matter which rhythm the band offers her, she has her own way of moving and it's with him, his sensitivity and sensuality, as if nothing else matters, only their entwinement.

The tingle of excitement under her skin slowly changes to a creeping numbness. They dance beyond the warmth of the hall. The grass is damp beneath her feet. Above their heads, the sky. Purple clouds have gathered, masking the moon and, for a moment, Astrid trembles. But there's nothing to be afraid of. Close by other couples are dancing. All the girls are dressed in white as she is and all the men in black. The men are also clasping their partners closely as if intending never to let them free.

She's in a dream, no, not a dream, a fairy story, where she has no mother or father; she's a lost orphan waiting to be found, to be claimed. But is her man a benevolent prince or the devil himself?

Astrid feels herself being bent one way and another, as if having no free will. She's lost control over her own body. Her partner's now a wiry, strong creature, with fingers that hold hers so tightly she knows the blood is being squeezed from her heart. Her eyes are suddenly dazzled by a bright flash of colour. Her virgin's dress is transformed to a scarlet shift. The brazen shimmer of the fabric fills her with an excitement she has never known before, a searing pleasure-pain which tingles her limbs, forces her breath to come in short bursts and fill her cheeks with a harlot's joy. She has no choice. Commanded by her once secret lust, she gives herself to him, lets him do what he wants with her, master her, control her.

She hears his whisper, 'I want you.'

She gasps.

'Not here,' he says. 'I will take you to another place where no one can reach us.'

She's no longer as she was. The former Astrid in the white dress is standing alone, abandoned. And another figure, a woman, old and gaunt, dressed in black, is there too, her hands held together in prayer as if to convey that it's too late.

But it isn't all over, is it? She can still hear the music coming from the hall, all the time faster and faster so that she can no longer keep track of what her feet are doing. And she loves her garish dress. The badge of her re-birth, her shameless self. How she glorifies in the person she has become. She wants more and more of the passion which fills her, of the man's fingers digging into her flesh, of his lips against her ears, his voice penetrating her. 'I have you, I have you.'

And she whirls against him, faster and faster, more frantic and even more so, losing her breath, losing her very soul to the moment, letting herself be absorbed into his body, until, suddenly, it is all over and he lets her drop to the cold ground.

The Young Man
with the Dog

'Fay, are you listening to me? Open your eyes.'

Fay nodded, not opening her eyes. She didn't want to listen nor talk, not even to her husband, especially not to him

'We need bread and bottled water. Can you manage that? There's money here, by the bed.'

She stayed silent.

He stood in the doorway, insistent. 'Are you going to the Hermitage? We have that reception on Friday. I don't know which entrance to use. Can you find out?'

When she didn't reply he left, slamming the outer door and turning the lock three times: clunk, clunk, clunk.

Fay rolled into the middle of the warm bed, pushing her face against the pillows, hugging her body, prodding her empty stomach, knowing hunger would eventually force her up and out into the cold street. Until then she didn't want to wake up, didn't want to see the gloomy room which would not lighten even when she drew back the curtains. She didn't want to be in St Petersburg, didn't want to be an appendage to a business deal, to be alone all day, waiting for her husband's return, waiting to be taken out to eat as if she were still a child. But, like a child who has woken too early, she went back to sleep until disturbed.

-◄◄◄•►►►-

A dog's bark woke her. The walls between the apartments were thin. Fay wondered whether anyone had heard them making love last night.

'I do love you, Fay,' he'd mumbled against her ear. 'You won't be disappointed.'

That she *was* disappointed was her fault. She should never have married him. She hadn't been honest with him. Still single at thirty-five, she had wanted him for his money, for security. Her love was a sham; she was deceiving him.

A line of yellowing light where the curtains didn't meet let her read the clock, hanging high on the bedroom wall. Ten o'clock. Her self-appointed getting up time. But Fay didn't move, for what was the rush? It would take her ten minutes, fifteen at the most, to shop at the supermarket across the street and then what? Another visit to the Hermitage?

The minute they'd arrived in Russia her husband had said. 'I'll buy a Friends ticket. There's so much to see. Most tourists get half a day at the most. You're lucky.'

He was right, of course. She should be appreciative. She wasn't a tourist. She had two weeks to visit the Hermitage. If she wanted to.

A man's voice shouted in Russian and the dog stopped barking. On the landing outside their apartment a door opened, boot studs and claws grated against the concrete floor and the door was slammed. As the key clanked inside the lock, a television sent harsh music through the wall and the old man coughed.

'I saw a rather unsavoury character on the way in,' her husband had said the day before. 'Elderly.'

'With a beard, wearing a blue cap and glasses?'

'He was hanging round outside our door.'

'He was getting his breath back after climbing four flights of stairs,' Fay said. 'He lives in the next apartment. I've seen him taking the dog out.' After a short pause she added, 'He doesn't live alone.'

'He's bound to have a wife.'

'I've heard a second voice. A man's.' Younger than you, she thought, but she didn't say it. Her thoughts were her own.

-⟨⟨⟨◆⟩⟩⟩-

She pushed back the cheap bedcover, a kind of thin, stiff duvet, too narrow for a double bed but they'd turned it round, not fretting that their feet were uncovered, felt for her slippers and stood between the bed and the window.

Tugging the curtain back, she saw the same as she'd seen the last four mornings, since her husband had brought her to this city, this foreign place. Their apartment was at the top of the building, the triangle of space between the roofs filled with a grey sky. The wall opposite was too close and full of square windows, either curtained or dull reflections of nothing. Even on tiptoe she could not glimpse the ground, not a pebble of the small courtyard which she knew was there.

It must be like this in prison. Do the prisoners look into the windows opposite and imagine what is happening in rooms identical to theirs? Do they strain to listen to sounds on the other side of the wall? Do they imagine who owns the voices?

For Fay did. Ever since she heard the second voice in the apartment next door and realized it was not the voice of the old man who coughed but of a younger, more virile man, she wondered what he was like. Was he thin-necked and scrawny like his father? Or was he tall and big shouldered like the army officers who stamped the streets in their brown top coats, their faces inscrutable under the peaks of their flat hats? Did he have a girl? If so, she wouldn't be one of the up-to-the-minute variety, with a fur coat and boots. He wouldn't have the money for one of those. Maybe she'd be one of the cheap, flashy kind, all lipstick and short skirts and bold, brash laughter. Surely not a meek girl, shabbily dressed in a thin denim jacket? He deserved better than that.

But she must not think of the young Russian. She must obey her husband: buy bread and water and investigate the arrangements for this reception.

There were no windows on the stairway of the block. To get electric light she must press a square metal plate on the wall, with its minute red eye, awake twenty-four seven. First she must put on her boots, stained with dry snow and street slush, unlock the front door with her hall light still on, leave the door swinging while she switched the light off and then go onto the landing, press the plate, pull the door to and turn the heavy key in the lock. Clunk, clunk, clunk.

A scrabble of claws and scrape of boots. He was coming up the stairs. The man with the dog. Not the old man because he was back there, coughing. Suddenly, their heads were level. They both stared. She supposed he was taking in her blond hair, her navy wool coat, her lack of fur, not even a collar made from fox to compete with the local women. He was maybe in his late twenties, tall and broad with slanted brows, slate-blue eyes, a large nose and high, dramatic cheekbones under smooth skin. The leather jacket and fur hat she would have expected.

Neither spoke. She blushed and looked down. As they reached the landing, the dog whined, sniffing at the cracks where the walls met the floor finding the usual stench of grimy boots and stale urine. The man tugged at the lead and stepped round her. Her pulse ticked.

He was nothing like his father, not at all an old man who understood married life. Refusing to consider whether the son had known a woman and understood the noises she had made the previous night, Fay held onto the metal hand-rail as she walked down the stairs.

In the street, the icy wind caught her. She pulled up the collar of her coat and, her moral superiority banished to warmer climes, wished for a fur hat. Setting her face in the hard, bleak expression which, she knew, would protect her against petty theft, she marched along Nevsky Prospekt. The great, coloured baubles heralding the festive season did their best but the people on the pavement shoved her aside and ignored her.

None of the inhabitants of St Petersburg knew how to smile. It wasn't that they glared, just looked glum, their mouths straight lines, their eyes saying, 'You're a foreigner. I can tell by your clothes, by your handbag, by the way you walk, by the way you think you can smile at me.' Unless they were shop assistants who stared past you as their expression said, 'You won't buy anything, you're only looking.'

She shopped in the glaring lights of the basement shop, its shelves stacked high with pickled herrings, gherkins and rye bread, flour and cooking oil. Going home, the huge, plastic drum of water was heavy, but a necessity. Tap water was unsafe. Too late she remembered her obligation to visit the Hermitage. Like a tourist. Tomorrow would do. Culture was no cure for the wild adventures invading her head.

The image of the young man with his wolf nose walked ahead of her. She was light-headed. She should have eaten before coming out. Now greed stabbed at her insides, one of the lusts of the flesh easily satisfied.

At the confectionery shop, she bought a slice of gateau, a slab of tempting coffee-flavoured cake, layered and crusted with icing and walnuts. The memory of her young Russian gave her an appetite, a desire for indulgence. Instead of taking the cake back to the flat, to eat hastily sitting at the chipped, formica-topped table in the cramped kitchen, she ordered a hot chocolate, Italian style, and sat at one of the round, marble-topped tables, sipping the creamy drink. She ate her luscious cake and then ordered a second mug of chocolate and a honey cake to take away, not caring that her stomach would curve outwards, like that of a Rubens woman, that her insides would be cloyed with hot sweetness.

Back in the flat she sank onto the bed and slept in her clothes like a slut.

'Did you get the bread for my breakfast?' her husband asked later.

'I bought a cake too,' she told him. 'Now and then I need a treat, something to sustain me in this cold, wintery place.'

-‹‹‹◆›››-

The next day Fay wandered through the great green building of the Winter Palace, looking at the rooms rather than what was in them: at the painted ceilings, the blue and red and brown swirls on the cream and white. At the floors: the patterns made by eighteen different kinds of wood cut and fitted together, nature's jigsaw. At the trompe l'oeil: the grey shaded painting pretending to be elaborate plaster columns and cornices. Hours passed. Fatigued with looking, she ignored the relics from Before Christ and the Egyptian trophies and walked through open double doors, round corners, following signs printed with directional arrows as if she knew where she was heading.

A large sign informed her the Treasury was open. In front of a pair of shut doors was a desk, protected by a red cord barrier. Three attendants sat behind the desk not smiling.

Fay didn't smile either. 'The Treasury?'

'Special ticket,' said one of the women hardly moving her lips.

Fay held out her Friend's membership card. 'Will this do?' She knew the woman couldn't understand exactly what she was saying but suddenly she felt determined to achieve this, to see what was inside the Treasury, to make the woman open the doors for her.

The woman glanced at the plastic, heaved herself to her feet and unhooked the red cord barrier. 'Sign,' she ordered, pushing a book across the desk. Scowling as if this was the very last thing she'd expected to do, the woman unlocked one of the doors.

Fay walked through into four rooms boasting riches. The trophies of the great and the good of the past: the golden bowls and cups and plate. The silver swords and the rewards of the not so good: rubies, emeralds and sapphires glistened under chandeliers. More wealth than she ever imagined under one roof. More wealth than she ever believed owned by Russia; more wealth than she believed should have been owned by certain establishments, she thought, staring at a bishop's hat, sewn with a thousand seed pearls. All hers to wonder at for as long as she wanted, quite alone. The silence of the place was the silence of a great vault, the silence of hidden deeds, of secret jealousies, of repressed lusts.

She was examining a headdress made from figured gold leaves, twisted together with a fine stalk, so slender you'd have thought the metal would have snapped, when a man's footstep, heavy in boots walking through from the last room, startled her. Someone was in here with her, had been there, in the next room, all the time. Guessing he was a guard, refusing to turn round, she moved to the next display: two exquisite gold earings, their detail so intricate a magnifying glass had been placed over them. The step moved with her.

How ridiculous. What did he think, that she intended to smash the glass of the case and snatch the jewellery? Daring herself not to be intimidated, she turned to confront her spy. And blushed and blinked and felt stupid. She was facing the young man from the next-door apartment.

In his navy uniform and without his hat he looked beautiful, chiselled hard. But cold. She tried smiling, just a 'hello, we do know each other' but his lips didn't move. Ridiculously hurt, she ignored him and walked to a case containing eighteenth century English artefacts. He kept in pace with her, close behind her. She gazed on a manicure set in its marcasite case while her imagination was full of the man behind her, the man who lived and slept on the other side of the wall. The man who would not smile at her. How she wished she had put on just a dash of lipstick; longed not to be invisible.

Her pleasure was spoiled. She left the Treasury without saying 'Goodbye' for what was the point? She thanked the women at the desk and they blinked 'What for?' back at her. She shivered, cold and empty.

On the way home she visited the patisserie to eat choux pastry and cream with her sundowner, assuring herself that her husband would like her full, soft body, her seductive curves, her new fleshiness.

That night she rolled across the mattress to him and whispered words of love and lust in his ear while she thought of her Russian. She shut herself in her head and thought of the young man, seeing him lie above her, feeling him touch her. She opened her mouth and tasted him, licked that smooth skin. She hoped he could hear her through the wall, could hear her passion. Could hear she was able to teach him about love. When she slept she dreamed of him, of them together, lying on the floor of a room crammed with jewels.

The next morning her husband asked, 'Did you go to the Hermitage yesterday?'

She shook her head. 'I got as far as Palace Square but coachloads of Japanese were taking photos and small armies of school children were marching through the arch towards the Palace so I skipped it. I'll go today.'

-«««•»»»-

She dressed more carefully and put on lipstick before she went again to the Treasury to wander in the golden rooms. In the silence she waited for the heavy footsteps. When she heard them she turned immediately, smiling. To her dismay, he stared through her, lifted his head higher and looked at the wall, not even a glimmer of recognition on his face.

The rejection hurt as much as if her dream had already failed, as if her fantasies were just that. She felt bitter and didn't wait for more humiliation but left quickly. She longed for sugary sweetness, for the comfort of rich chocolate, for the sublime sense of luxury on her lips. On the way home she stopped at the coffee shop, sitting at one of the small tables, eating almond tart, drinking hot chocolate, French style, the melted stuff thick enough to spoon up, thick enough to satiate her.

-«««•»»»-

She was resting on her bed when she heard a commotion in the outside corridor. A voice was shouting from below and another, her young neighbour's, was calling out. He sounded agitated, alarmed. With her boots half zipped, she yanked open her front door.

He was standing on his threshold, wearing a white shirt and jeans, calling out harsh words. Words full of pain. When he saw Fay he said, 'Help me. I must get my father downstairs or they will leave.' He turned and went inside his own flat.

'Who will?' Fay followed him into his apartment and straight into a bedroom. On a narrow bed lay the old man.

'The men in the ambulance. They only drive. Not carry. We must get him downstairs.'

Ignorant of these things, Fay couldn't argue. She turned her back to the old man's stockinged feet, tucked his legs under her arms and helped lift him off the bed. She walked, face forward, down the stairs, not seeing the son, who was matching his steps with hers, waiting for his hands to turn the old man on the curve of the staircase, hearing him mutter softly, without knowing whether he was cursing her or blessing her. Together, they carried the father to the street door.

The men with the ambulance waited indolently as they took the patient right into the van, dropping him onto the bunk. Of course the son went with his father. Of course his concern for his father's condition made him forget to say either 'Thank you' or 'Goodbye'.

Two hours later, after the sun had set, when she opened the door, she didn't know whether she was more surprised by the sight of the young man or the bottle of vodka he was carrying.

He held up the bottle. 'I say, thank you.' Adding, if it made the difference, 'Please.'

'In here?' She held the door back. 'How is your father?'

'His heart very bad. He die.'

Her own shock seemed greater than his. Her hands shook as she put glasses on the kitchen table. He poured vodka, drank it and poured again.

Fay sipped and then drank, the liquid running down her throat so easily. Too easily. She'd be drunk. Apart from the cake, she hadn't eaten anything that day. What could she offer him? She opened the door of the fridge as if delicacies would appear by magic. There were some olives and a few slices of pale cheese with holes in. The bread was a slab of cold, baked mud, spotted with small, hard grains of rye.

'Shall we sit down?' She led the way into the sitting room, generous with its two settees and three armchairs. In here the windows were draped with red velvet and the lamps glowed a flattering, candle yellow. She sat at the end of a settee, still holding her glass, watching him eat and drink.

He sat next to her, his weight pressing the seat flat, pouring more from the bottle and saying, 'Drink. It is the only way of keeping warm.'

Was he so cold he didn't notice the central heating? It was enough to make you sweat but she couldn't turn it off or down, only open windows which he might find uncomfortable. The room smelt of her scent and his body.

He re-filled their glasses, slopping wetness onto the brocade covered cushion. 'You from England?'

She felt his breath too close, couldn't help watching his lips move, his fingers curl around the glass. 'Yes.'

'You stay long?' He finished his drink and filled his glass again and then hers.

She gulped the vodka, no longer noticing the sting in her throat, no longer wondering what she was doing, getting drunk with this beautiful, cold man, this man she longed to touch? 'We go home at the end of next week.'

The bottle was empty. The cheese and olives eaten. They waited together in a heat enough for them both to be naked.

At last Fay said, 'What will you do now? About the funeral?' She wished she could help, to offer to make sandwiches, to order flowers as she would have done for a neighbour at home.

When he stood, she swayed to her feet, standing too close, feeling too dizzy to care. He kissed her swiftly before she could reach out and hold onto his arm. Tasting salty cheese and bitter olives, more potent than cake and chocolate. She rocked on her feet, inviting him to hold her, too tightly, too urgently.

He kissed her again, greedily, as if the consequence had been agreed between them.

'No,' she said when she could. 'It's too late. My husband will be home soon.'

Had she said that? What did she mean? That she was prepared to make her fantasies reality? That she was already his? It was only a matter of time?

'You drink too much vodka,' he said. 'You must sleep.'

How kind of him. She would. She would sleep now and do it later. Tomorrow she would let him take her. He deserved it. She deserved it.

'You come to the Treasury tomorrow?'

'Of course.'

That determined it. At the Treasury he would speak to her and they would come home together and make love. Beautifully. She would not need to buy cake or warm herself with chocolate tomorrow.

-◄◄◆►►-

The woman on the desk did not trouble herself to push the book to her for signing and Fay walked straight into the Treasury. This morning she was not alone. A party of policemen were examining the displays. A guide was lecturing them. There was no sign of her lover. Her heart thumped with disappointment and settled into bored acceptance. She walked through to the last room and looked at four enamelled and decorated swords hanging in a huge case on the wall. They did not interest her at all. She was only interested in her guard, her very own security man.

The other party left the rooms and Fay tried to choose an item which she could describe to her husband later; to prove she was using her time wisely even though she wished otherwise, wished she was lying with another man, trading her body for a few moments of splendour.

A man's footstep made her whirl round. Not the right one. He was small and thin, wearing such scruffy clothes she wondered why the gorgon had let him in. Surely the authorities wanted to keep people like that out? She stared at a small box of ivory and mother-of-pearl, ignoring him.

Until he stood beside her. 'Give me money.'

In English.

'What money?'

'You a tourist. Rich. Give me money.'

'I don't have any.'

'Every day you buy cake. Give me money to buy bread and I go. I have a knife.'

What could she do? There was no one to help her. No security guard, not one she knew or one she didn't. The man pressed against her, his palm against her hip. She wanted to swoon, to pretend helplessness but then he might take her bag; her engagement and her wedding rings which were suddenly so precious. Fumbling, she took out her purse and opened it. 'There,' she whimpered. She felt so stupid, so taken advantage of. 'This is all I have.' She thrust a handful of notes at him, perhaps five hundred roubles, enough for food for a month for him, not enough to buy a bottle of wine for her.

He stuffed the money in his pocket and left the room.

She was trembling. What could she do? Complain to the woman on the desk? No. Go home. That was it. Go straight home and stay there until her husband returned.

And then he came to her. Walking slowly through the rooms, her special guard came to her rescue. 'You're here.'

He shrugged. 'So?'

'I've been robbed.'

'Robbed?'

'Yes. A man made me give him all my money. He said he had a knife. Why didn't you come?'

'What man?'

'He has gone.'

'I know of no man. You are alone here.'

She blinked fast. She didn't understand. She refused to cry. Tears were weak. She would not be weak in front of him. 'He was in here. Ask the woman on the desk.'

'The woman on the desk told me you were alone.' He stared above her head at the wall.

'She was lying.'

'Why would she lie?' Still he refused to look at her

Were they all in this together? The woman, the thief and her security guard? She stepped closer to him and begged. Placing a hand on his arm she said, 'Don't turn me away. I helped you.'

He shrugged again. 'That was nothing. My father was old.'

He doesn't want to know me, Fay thought. Has he forgotten? But she couldn't ask. Could not say the words, 'You kissed me.' Could not even think the words, 'I wanted to give myself to you.' Tears came then and she let them, not caring they belittled her. He was refusing her, shredding her dreams, tarnishing her desires.

She gave him time to take her and hold her, time which he did not use. She humiliated herself completely by sobbing, by pulling a hankie from her pocket and scrubbing her cheeks dry, scrubbing away her makeup, her shiny, sexy lipstick, while he stamped his feet impatiently and clenched his hands behind his back. When she had composed herself, she left him, left him in his kingdom, among his treasures and riches. Holding her head high, she stalked past the woman at the desk, through the rooms of the museum, past the glories of the past, the treasure of time gone.

Outside, Fay walked quickly across the vast space of Palace Square and through the cold streets of the city. She was wretched, behaving as a smitten schoolgirl. She was a fool. She had no dreams, no romantic fantasies, no money. She couldn't even buy cake or chocolate for comfort. She had no self-respect. She had nothing.

Suddenly, in the midst of her misery, she remembered her promise to her husband, her obligation. She would have to return to The Hermitage, to ask one of the haughty women on the desk what she needed to know.

It was now late afternoon but she turned and weaved her way through the street crowds back into The Hermitage. Do not send him, she prayed. Do not let him see me waiting. I couldn't bear it. She found out what she had to and she escaped, back to her tiny flat.

-«««◆»»»-

'Did you go to The Hermitage today?'

'Yes.' Her answer was a whisper.

'Did you enjoy it?'

'Yes.' She had no other answer. It was her duty to enjoy the opportunities she had. Her duty to please her husband. She had nothing else.

'Did you find out about the reception?'

'Yes.'

'Good. You'll enjoy it.'

'Yes.' She paused but she knew he didn't keep count. 'I need more money.'

He threw a handful of notes on the bed. 'After the reception we'll go to dinner. Don't eat too much cake.'

'I won't eat any.'

-«««◆»»»-

The next afternoon, she bathed and washed her hair, brushed it until it shone, dressed and made up her face. She etched seductive shadows on her eye-lids, furred her lashes and smoothed a lipstick smile on her lips. Her husband would be proud of her.

It was a glamorous event, an icon of glasnost. Drinking Georgian champagne and holding a plate of smoked salmon, Fay felt secure. Her body was sheened with velvet, her rounder hips and stomach promised soft excitement, her bare arms glowed warm, as if already pleasured. The gem, chained, against her neck was worthy of any Treasury.

Her husband approached anyone speaking English to swap information on business projects and rates of exchange. Every word he spoke made money. Amy ate and sipped and ate some more, smiling to herself as the waiters presented her with little cold blancmanges and mousses, thinking of her afternoon cake and her promise to indulge herself with sweets and hot chocolate every day.

A party of four men, in black suits, walked towards her, all tall with smooth hair, high cheekbones and firm mouths set in tense lines. All cold and calm. Security guards. While she gazed, made slow by too much alcohol, her neighbour smiled at her, bowing his head.

She returned his acknowledgment coldly victorious. She was the guest, he merely the servant. She flushed, triumphant he was seeing her while she was beautiful enough to be noticed, desirable but rich enough not to need to be wanted. She was being wooed by Russia, being feted, a Madonna in this newly open country where he was of no consequence.

She turned towards her husband.

Finishing

You never know what will tip them over the brink, bring the emotion out. You'd think my calling was full of tears and handkerchiefs, a real weepy, the ladies especially crying on my shoulders, but that's not how it is, at least to start with.

I remember we had a woman come in recently. We'd collected her mother a couple of days earlier. Lovely lady she'd been, I could see that. Good bones, deep set eyes, fully curved lips, even though they'd been drained of colour.

The daughter, fuller in the figure than her mother, with a very determined mouth, had brought in the clothes for the body. Over her arm she carried a smart black wool dress and jacket. Quality, the ensemble was. Already I could see the corpse dressed, looking her old self. I don't like to see them in a well-worn nightie, sometimes almost threadbare, as if the family had kept back her good stuff. Undignified. It's my job to give the dead back their self-respect even if they are in a higher place, one where no one worries about that sort of thing. I took the dress and jacket and hung it behind the door.

The daughter reached into a carrier bag, one of those environmental linen ones, and brought out a few bits of underwear and a pair of tights. I almost smiled. Usually the bereaved forget what's to go underneath, but not this one, she was the thorough type. She blushed though, as she handed them over.

Reaching again into her bag she said, 'These are her shoes. Red court. My mother wore them to parties.'

She said the word 'parties' with a perfectly straight face. Her eyes did not look at me but stared at the shoes, fixed on them as if she had only just discovered them, had never watched them taking her mother to parties.

I've trained my face not to betray me, my eyebrows don't lift with amazement nor my lips in amusement but I had to point out that the shoes didn't match the dress.

The daughter pretty much snapped at me. 'Matching never bothered her. It won't now.'

You never know what people will say.

Finally, she thrust her hand into the bag and pulled out a string of beads. 'I'd like her to wear this.'

'This' was a jet and marcasite necklace: long, 1920s style. Classy. Stylish. Like the black suit. Some would say it was a waste to bury it, but not me. It is the last rites, after all, and I reckon after living this hard life, a person deserves the best.

She gave me the beads, slipping them from her fingers to mine. Keeping her distance. 'I'd like her to look…'

'Finished?' I suggested. Finishing was what we do best at Winston & Winston.

'Will you…?' Again she hesitated.

They often do. Hesitate that is. In these days of explicit television, pornographic videos and X-rated manuals from book clubs, people still find it difficult to actually talk about 'it'.

Refusing to look me in the face, she asked, 'Will you be looking after her?'

Her skin coloured up again and I knew she was referring to the dressing of the body. I understood her discomfort. Who'd want to think of their own mother being seen naked by a strange man even if it was in a professional capacity? I hurried to reassure her. 'Not me. My wife takes care of that side of things. For the ladies, naturally.'

'Naturally.'

'Will you be in to see your mother?'

'I'll ring, shall I and see if you… if you're wife has…?'

'Finished.'

She left, banging the door behind her as if she was cross. It was odd, but I had the feeling she had something else to say, something she was finding difficult. That often happens. Usually with important matters. Important to the living, that is.

So I wasn't surprised when she turned up the following day, carrying a plastic carrier bag. When she spoke it was in a blurt, a rush of words, and her mouth trembled while her eyelids blinked. 'I don't know what to do with these.'

From the bag she pulled a pair of black boots and held them up. The soles were peeling at the toes although the heels looked freshly shod. The leather of the uppers was split in a couple of places, the laces were broken and knotted together.

'I can't bear to throw them in the bin.' She tried laughing but it was a thin, high noise. Forced.

I didn't understand. Hadn't she given me the courts? 'Do you want her to wear them?'

'No. She wouldn't. She'll be dressed for an occasion. These were for every day. She wore them every day. I tried to get her to buy a new pair once but she wouldn't. She could be quite difficult, my mother.'

As she delivered her little speech, a choke in her throat interrupted her words and her lashes blinked very quickly. I felt a cup of tea was in order.

When tea is necessary, we take our clients into the back room, away from the office with the door straight onto the street. It's personal business we deal in, very private, and often a little chat in peace and quiet can help matters along.

I brought the tea on a tray, the full works: tea-pot, two cups and saucers, milk in a little jug and sugar in a bowl. Often our clients are the mug and tea-bag type. This woman was definitely the china pot sort if not the full Royal Worcester.

'It's not uncommon to have the odd difference with a parent,' I began. 'Especially as the years get on.' I laughed. 'Reckon I can be tricky now and again.'

The daughter refused sugar and gave a heavy sigh. 'Mother should have let me buy her a new pair of boots. I suggested it but Mother rolled her lips together so I knew what she was going to say.'

'And what was that?' I prompted gently.

'That it was a ridiculous suggestion and she was having none of it. There's nothing wrong with these, that's what she said. Nothing wrong with them? They were falling to bits.' She sipped at her tea. 'Mother said she could fix the peeling uppers with glue and the cracks in the leather would fill in nicely with a bit of blacking. She told me her mother said, 'I bought them from that shop at...' The daughter bit her lip as if she didn't want to talk about the boots any more. Apart from muttering that her mother had told her the boots would last a lifetime.

I tried a little joke. 'In a way they did.' Which was ignored.

'She had the nerve to accuse me of being bossy. As I told her, I was only trying to help.'

'What did she say to that?'

'That she'd prefer the help of a gin and tonic.'

I laughed. 'I'm partial to a G and T myself.'

'But it was half-past three in the afternoon.'

'I expect she watched one of those quiz programmes on the television?'

The daughter gave me a sharp look. 'She did as it happens.'

'It gets to be a habit with us older ones. Did you take her shopping?'

She nodded. 'I took her back to the West End. I have to admit even I found the experience confusing.

She described the shoe shop window in some detail. I could feel my eyes glazing over. Until she finished with, 'I thought we came for boots, Mum said. And then back in the far corner of the window, as though someone had added them as an afterthought, were a pair of brown, lace-up boots.'

'And?'

The daughter looked down into her cup before telling me a long story about a disagreement she'd had with her mother in the shop. Until the shop girl asked her mother if she'd like to try the boots on.

Her voice was beginning to get to me but it's my job to listen. For however long.

'Mum said, I will if you want me to but I'm not buying them. I don't need new boots. It's my daughter who thinks I do, but it's not my daughter paying, is it? I don't like brown. Do you force your mother to wear things she doesn't want?'

By the time she stopped for breath her voice had a dry catch in it.

'More tea?' I offered.

She held out her cup. 'Mum wouldn't buy the boots. She told me her old ones were the most comfortable shoes she'd ever worn. She said in a loud voice, in front of everyone in the shop, I can manage. I don't need you. Then she marched out of the shop with me trying to keep up, rummaged in her bag for her bus pass and jumped on the next bus home.'

The daughter pressed her lips against the cup and drank, frantically, as if the warm liquid would give her the strength to deal with her dead mother. She was upset, much more than she wanted me to see.

I cleared my throat before I said carefully, 'They don't mean it. I bet your mother was proud of having a daughter like you.'

'I did love her, you know.' She sounded strained, tired. 'I only wanted the best for her, just as she's always given me the best. I just wanted to show I loved her. I just wish Mother had let me help her. To think we quarrelled over a pair of boots. If only I could chuck the wretched things in the bin but I can't, I just can't.'

I felt sorry for her then and stood up. 'Leave the boots with me. I've an idea.'

-◄◄◄◆►►►-

When the daughter came to see her mother the day before the funeral, she looked ill, pale and tense. I could see it was a shock for her to see her mother laid out. Our chapel of rest is not large and, for the visitor, it's as though there's nowhere to put yourself. That moment when they walk across the threshold, that's the reckoning. There's no escape. The space is full of death.

I was pleased with the result. Old people are tricky. Too many wrinkles to be tucked. They can end up with a caustic expression which even makeup can't obliterate. This one had smooth skin which took a sweep of colour on the cheeks very nicely and enough hair to puff up bouffant style. It was a shame about the mouth. By the time I'd taken out the false teeth and stitched up the lips, the curves were tightened and I had only a thin a line to follow for the lipstick.

The daughter stood with her back pressed against the wall for a moment or two but then took a deep breath and stepped closer to the coffin. She bent over the body and stroked her mother's hand. A gentle gesture, full of affection but when her own fingers touched the cold flesh, she drew back sharply. That always surprises people. They read about 'cold as marble' but they don't believe it.

The hand, which I had balanced finely on the hip, slipped and fell. While I picked it up and resettled it higher on the chest, almost touching the necklace, the daughter asked me what I had done with the boots.

'Her boots? They're tucked in here, in the coffin.'

'I'd like to see.'

Which told me she didn't trust me but I didn't take offence. You never know how a death will affect people.

Carefully, I pulled back the white lace covering the lower half of the coffin, revealing the black wool skirt and two thin, bone-white calves. 'There, see, they just fit.'

The daughter looked at the boots settled in between her mother's legs, just above her feet shod in the red court shoes.

'Thank you,' she said. 'I wish she knew she'd still got them with her. It would make her smile.'

And turning her face away from her mother's body, she began to sob.

Which made me feel better. They need to cry. You never can tell what will finish it.

Afterword

Novels are grown-up friends, often with firm personalities. The writer is engaged with them frequently and the relationship develops into a history.

Short stories are children; they arrive unformed, as a fleeting idea, and often unbidden. They take years of nurture, several drafts reflecting their development and then give back joy and relief when they are complete.

Here's the background to each story.

Dressed for a Party & Finishing. These two stories, about my mother's death, form 'bookends' for the collection. *Dressed for a Party* is an example of life writing, drafted soon after my mother had died. I needed to clear my head of some aspects of the painful business of a family death. Later, for personal amusement, I wrote *Finishing* from the viewpoint of the funeral director. I like the way this story ends on a positive note.

A Fish out of Water was written while I was following a Creative Writing MA at Chichester University. The module was on Metaphor & the Imagination. I took my imagination back to an Italian villa where we'd enjoyed a summer holiday. Apart from deciding to use the rule of 3 by giving my narrator three children, I have no idea where the various ideas sprang from, apart from analysing all aspects of the location, adding metaphor and imagination and an admiration for Angela Carter. The story won a prize.

Blood Red Berries is a blending of a trip we took to South America, a couple we met on another holiday and my early love of the narrative voices in the stories of W Somerset Maugham. The narrator speaks in an old fashioned manner; one I heard when a child.

The blood red berries, seen on a walk, were pointed out by the guide as poisonous and we were warned not to touch them.

The Assumption grew from my amusement at discovering a grave stone in a French cemetery, with the husband's name and date of death, together with the name of his wife and a blank where her date of death would eventually be carved. That curious custom, made me think of the woman living with that reminder that she must die. I put her to live in the house next to the cemetery, owned by good friends of ours, added the French obsession with food, my love of angels on graves and a twist.

Conflict is a very personal story. Our son fought in the Iraq war. The story, dating from 2003, is the simple truth. I first wrote this story from my point of view. Too sentimental. I changed the narrator to the father. Couldn't write it. But as the grandfather – once I'd killed off the parents of the soldier boy – the words arrived.

The Magic Answer is also in the magical realism genre. I was following a week's writing course on an atmospheric Greek island. In my spare time I explored the landscape, discovering the steep hill surrounding the barren pit. The place gave me dark ideas. I wrote in the contemporary voice of a thirties-something woman who didn't want to become a mother and, with research, added details from Greek mythology.

Old Skin and Cabbage. This story goes back years to when I regularly visited my mother-in-law in her care home. My husband can't hear as well as he once could and we'd attended a presentation at London Zoo from a company selling hearing aids. To this knowledge of care homes plus the challenge to everyone who has poor hearing, I added the fact that a short temper comes to us all in the end. And I'm a fan of jigsaws.

The Dance was inspired by two paintings by Munch, *Girls on the Pier* and *The Dance of Life,* seen at an art gallery in Norway. The story comes out of putting the two paintings together.

The Young Man and the Dog is part autobiography. During two years of our life my husband worked part-time in St Petersburg. I joined him now and then. We became Friends of The Hermitage but, for most weekdays, I was in our flat, writing or shopping for food. The idea came from a newspaper article reporting that ambulances would come as far as the inner courtyard of a block of flats, but the medics refused to climb the stairs to carry a sick person down on a stretcher. Apart from the hot chocolate and the cakes, the rest is a confection.

Also by Jane Hayward

The Baby Box

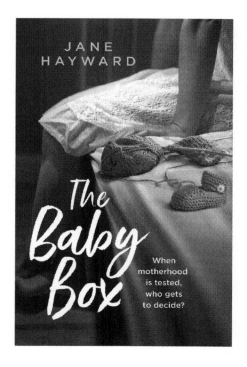

Jane Hayward's memoir *The Baby Box* is a frank and compelling narrative, set in the 1960s. A true story, kept secret for fifty years.

 Matador

For exclusive discounts on Matador titles,
sign up to our occasional newsletter at
troubador.co.uk/bookshop